ONE YEAR STAND WITH A PHILLY BILLIONAIRE 2

YONA

One Year Stand With A Philly Billionaire 2

Copyright © 2023 by Yona

All rights reserved.

Published in the United States of America.

Published by Cole Hart Signature, LLC.

Mailing List

To stay up to date on new releases, plus get information on contests, sneak peeks, and more,

Go To The Website Below...

www.colehartsignature.com

CHAPTER ONE

AMARIE

Kasha and I were on our way back after I had finally moved a family into a house. I was excited to know that I would soon start seeing some money. It would be all mine and not tied to anyone. I was jumping for joy and couldn't wait to take my cousins out to eat and share the good news. Once I made enough, I would take them on a trip, all on me. I owed them that much.

"You the shit, and since the house is paid off, you should open an account for if you ever need to send out someone to fix some shit. That's what I do just so I'm not coming out of pocket," Kash said.

"Okay, I'll make one tomorrow," I agreed.

I always took his advice and listened. Never once did I try to make it my way or cheat through it. I did each step and worked my ass off to get where I belonged.

"What you gon' do as far as ole boy?" Kash asked a question he'd never asked before.

"I've applied online for the papers. The next step is to see if the judge approves it. I don't have a lawyer, so I'll probably have to get one when they bring us in. You know, like a court-appointed one," I explained.

"You can represent yourself or find yourself some kind of legal help. But they will not give you a lawyer," he replied, making me feel dumb.

"I guess I'll look more into that."

He nodded and continued driving toward his house.

"And what about all your things?"

"Who knows? I don't want to go to that house. I may just start over. I also thought about not taking any more time off from my job and not even quitting until I'm making enough money from these houses," I admitted.

"What if we changed some of the rules in this one year? How 'bout I pay for all your stuff, so you don't have to work? You just have to continue being who you are and keep giving me that good stuff."

"I'm down. Shit, when you want me to put my notice in?" I asked.

He laughed and grabbed my face, then kissed me. I let his tongue glide into my mouth. Sucking on it lightly, I let out a low moan. Then I let my hand slide up and down his length, gripping him in the process.

"You gon' suck him?" he questioned with his eyes low.

Kash pulled the car over, calling my bluff.

I grinned. That was all he needed to say. Anything he wanted, I had him. I released him from his pants and sucked him into my mouth. My head bobbed slowly up and down, not missing a beat. I kept a steady rhythm for a while to build him up. Then I teased him by licking all over his dick like I was giving him a tongue bath.

Finally, I took him into my mouth at the same time as I gently massaged his balls. Looking up into his eyes, I held his gaze as I slowly slurped him back into my mouth, using my tongue to stimulate the head. I switched back and forth between sucking and licking, taking him as far into my mouth as possible without choking.

Closing my eyes, I steadied my breathing and slowly eased down on him. I heard him suck in a breath, and his body tensed. I placed my hands in the praying position, guiding them up and down as I went to work. In seconds, he came in my mouth, and I swallowed his seeds.

"Climb on daddy's dick." Kash pulled me by my hands over the middle console and on top of him.

I looked out the window to see that he had pulled into one of the truck stops on the side of the highway.

"Come on, baby. Let me feel my warm pussy," he whispered in my ear just as he slid my panties to the side and inserted two fingers in me.

"Oh, yes," I moaned, sucking his neck.

He quickly lifted me and then set me down on his hard penis.

I closed my eyes, enjoying what felt like heaven on Earth to me as he held my hips and guided me the way he wanted me to go. I swayed my hips from side to side before rotating them in slow circles. I effortlessly began to bounce on him, driving him insane.

Kasha grunted and mumbled incoherent words while I rode him. He held onto my hips and lifted himself, slamming into me. I slowly eased up and down on it, squeezing my pussy muscles together. He groaned while grabbing my hips and pulling me down until he was fully inside me. I placed my feet on each side of him and then began to bounce up and down, causing him to let low moans leave his lips. We kissed slowly while he guided my hips at the pace he wanted.

"Fuckkkkkk," Kash dragged out longer than necessary.

I rotated my hips like I was dancing to a reggae song. Then,

I leaned back a little, placing both my legs onto his shoulders and pushing my hands into his lap. I started off at a slow pace, grinding into him back and forth, slow and steady. He placed his finger on my lips, and I sucked it into my mouth, moaning in the process.

"Ooh, daddy. Damn, I'm gon' cum!" I screamed as I came all over him.

Kasha slammed me down on him over and over until he filled me with his seeds. I stayed on his lap with my head against his chest. He placed a kiss on my forehead, then I climbed back in my seat and drifted off to sleep as he pulled off.

When Kash finally woke me up, we were in front of a restaurant.

"Come on, baby," he said and opened the door for me.

We walked hand in hand into the restaurant, and to my surprise, all my family was there. His dad was there with a white lady who was smiling very hard.

"Come on, let's go meet my parents." He pulled me over to them, and I was surprised that the lady was his mom. She was very beautiful, and when she opened her mouth, she reminded me of my auntie but with more class.

"Hey, baby, I'm his momma. You can call me Ma or Ms. Kristie." She pulled me into a hug, and I smiled.

"Nice to see you again, baby girl," his dad greeted me.

"Hello. Nice to see you again, too. I hope this place has food like your restaurant does," I admitted because I was hungry as hell.

"I hope so because this is my restaurant as well. I've met your cousins. They came in with his knuckle-headed friends. Where are your parents?" he asked.

"I don't know. I didn't even know we were coming here," I said because I didn't.

I was dressed in some damn skinny jeans and a button-down shirt. Of course, I had on a pair of cute little heels from Fashion Nova, though.

"Your shoes are amazing." I looked at his mom's red bottoms. They were to die for.

She had on the So Kate booties, and I loved them. I knew they cost about a thousand dollars. She also had a small Rolex watch that sat on top of a diamond bracelet. Her gray hair was curled to perfection, and red lipstick was on her lips like she had gotten her face beat right before the event.

"Girl, that man put it together for you," my auntie came over and spoke.

"Okay, this is my Auntie Ann. This is Kash's mom, Ms. Kristie, and this is his dad. Oh, and that's Kash." I pointed to everyone.

"How y'all doing? Y'all did y'all thing with that man. I'm glad he met my niece. She needed him in her life to help her see that life is better on the other side." My auntie sipped her drink.

"Yeah, he's a good man. I can't wait to get to know more about you. I'm glad we all could meet," Ms. Kristie said and took a sip of her wine.

What got me was when she pulled her weed from her bag and took a pull. She offered my auntie some, but she quickly declined and pulled out her own. I never knew my auntie to smoke with anyone, not even her own kids. She said people laced their weed all the time, and she didn't want any parts of that.

"I'm going to let y'all chat. I smell chicken," I said before going to look for the food.

My cousins and their dates were over at the tables. Nakari waved me over, but she would have to wait until I fixed my plate. When I saw the food, my mouth watered. I got a plate and filled it with mashed potatoes, chicken, and asparagus. I even went as far as getting some damn bread. Grabbing a cup, I filled it with the punch that sat halfway empty on the table before joining my cousins.

"Hey, everybody," I greeted before stuffing a fork full of food in my mouth.

"Girl, you know when Javon told me what Kash was trying to do, I had to help him set this dinner up. Your mom and dad are here somewhere, probably sitting back, watching them. You know, before they get comfortable, they have to make sure they can put they guns down."

I had to laugh because Natalia was right. My mom and dad's mindsets were always trained on military combat. They had to figure out all exits and entries of places like someone was after them. It used to get me mad, but now I just let them do them. Whatever kept them at peace was okay with me.

"You good, baby?" Kash whispered in my ear.

"Yeah, I'm good. Hungry as hell," I said as he snatched a buffalo wing off my plate.

I looked over and wanted to punch him. All that food on the table, and he wanted to eat mine.

"I'm about to go make me a plate. You want a drink?" he asked.

"Yeah, a Sex on the Beach," I told him.

Kash kissed my lips and walked away. I watched him with a smile on my face. That was a good man, and I was glad he was on my side. It would feel even better when he was all mine, and I was all his because fuck all the other stuff. That was a goal I had stored in my head, and it was long term too.

"Congrats on the houses. I ain't gon' lie. I was nervous for my boy, but I see how happy you make him, so I'm happy for y'all. Plus, I can't be on your bad side. Ya cousin too thorough, and you hang with her, so you got to be a good person as well," Von said.

"Thanks. I'm just taking things one day at a time. I know shit seems wrong, but I ain't trying to hurt him, and I ain't got no plans to move backward. It's up from here. We in this forever," I assured him.

"Bitch, get the fuck out of here with that mushy shit. We gangsters. All we know is free the mob," Nakari joked.

"Free the guys!" I laughed as we cheered.

Whatever was in the punch had me feeling good. As I looked around at everyone mingling, I smiled. This was what family was supposed to look like, and I loved the feeling.

CHAPTER TWO
AMARIE

"We got to do something with the family again. I really had fun," I told Kash as we walked into the house.

We had gone out to see a movie, which he fell asleep on. He kept saying he wasn't sleeping but was snoring hard and loud. I was ready to go sleep myself, but I needed to take a shower first.

"Why we ain't stop for food?" I asked because my stomach was growling.

"You said you wasn't hungry for the first time since I've known you. So, shit, I wasn't going to force you to eat. I was ready to take you anyway because I knew some shit like this would happen," he said as he kicked his shoes off.

"What you about to do? I think I'm going home tonight," I said.

I felt like I was starting to crowd his space. I never went home, and I was always under him.

"Home? You call the hotel home? You might as well stop paying for it," he said as someone knocked on the door.

"Who the fuck is that?" Kash asked as he swung the door open. It could have been some killers, and he didn't even check to see.

Looking over his shoulder, I found it weird that a girl was standing there. She was pretty too. Instead of saying anything, I stayed quiet. Who the hell was she? I knew I couldn't be mad if that was somebody he was fucking with, but in a way, I could because he knew everything I did and everything that came with me. While he was busy promising me the world, he had a bitch in the shadows.

"Amarie?" she said, and I stepped up because I didn't know the bitch.

"You've been served." She handed me papers, and I looked at them, knowing damn well no one was suing me.

If DeJuan wanted a divorce, he could have just signed the papers instead of going to great lengths to get to me.

Kash closed the door, and I ripped the papers open. It was a court summons. My mom was suing me to get a percentage of the building proceeds. I didn't understand why she played it cool with me if those were her intentions. Then, she wasn't even asking for the entire building back, but a percentage of profits instead. So, she wanted me to do all the work, and she reaped the benefits. I didn't care what kind of training she had; I wanted to knock her ass out.

Picking up my phone, I dialed her number twice, but she didn't answer. This bitch knew I would get the papers and was just around me like she wasn't plotting. I had confided in her, telling her every move I made when it came to the company because I wanted to make her proud, and the whole time, she was being a listening ear just so she could work up a way to get a cut.

"Look, whatever it is, don't cry about it. The shit isn't gon' happen. Just fight it," Kash said, but he didn't understand how fucked up this was.

"My mom is taking me to court for a percentage of the building and/or profits it makes. I'm not trying to give her that. Yeah, she gave me the building, but I put in all the footwork. She played in my face like she cared and like she wanted to be a mother when really, she was getting all her information to take me to court," I snapped.

"Shit like that happens. You have to know how to be the bigger person to get the outcome you want. Try to reach an agreement with her before you even get to court. Get it signed and notarized. That way, when you do get to that point, everything on your end looks good. You can give her something small. It won't hurt who you are going to become. Watch how shit plays out in your favor," he told me and kissed my forehead.

I heard what he said, but that didn't take away how I felt.

Kash grabbed my hand and led me upstairs. He walked to the bathroom and turned the shower on while I sat on the bed, thinking about what to do. Just when shit seemed to be going perfectly, things only got worse. I knew it couldn't get any worse than this. My day was going so well, and then she came and fucked it up. Some kind of parent. I didn't want anything to do with my mother, and if my dad was okay with her doing that, he could kiss my ass too.

"Come on, babe, before the water gets cold," Kash said as he stripped out of his clothes.

I followed suit, taking off my clothes and following him down the hall and into the bathroom.

I stepped into the shower and let the hot water hit my body. Kash grabbed me by my waist and pulled me back to him.

"Everything gon' be fine. You still got some time, anyway,

to make this year with a billionaire worth it. Yo' ass slipped up when you were drunk that night and talking to your cousins. You were all speaking on how this one year thing with a billionaire might not be so bad. We ain't even got through the first four months, and already, you wrapped up under me. Imagine if we make it to the year, and I do some crazy shit like put a baby in you. I need some leverage, so your ass don't try to leave me."

Kash placed soft kisses on my neck while his hands slowly slid all over my body. I lowly moaned, letting my head relax on his shoulder. I tilted it a little, so he could have more access.

He lifted my leg and placed it on the side of the shower. "Ooh," I softly let out as his fingers danced around on my pearl.

He slid his fingers back and forth between my clit and my opening, applying slight pressure when needed. Kash's finger slid inside me, causing me to gasp for air.

"My pussy wet for me, huh, baby?" he whispered in my ear right before he licked it.

He must have found a rhythm because he was finger fucking me and rubbing my clit in a circular motion all at once. The shit felt so good; I felt like I would pass out.

"Fuck, baby. Your pussy about to cum all over your fingers," I cried out in pleasure.

My breathing changed, and my hips moved against his fingers. He picked up his pace and had me creaming all over his digits. This man should have been called DJ the way he worked them fingers.

"My dick is really hard right now," he told me, and I giggled before turning around to look down at it.

The sight of that long rod had my mouth watering. I was dying to taste him and hear him groan in my ear.

Kash looked down at me and smiled. I smiled back as I eased down to my knees, ready to take him whole. I grabbed him in my hands, looking at him face to face. Right now, it was just him and me. Licking my lips, I opened my mouth and slowly took him in. I let my head go all the way down before pulling back up and making that popping sound when I let him go. I licked around his head, allowing my tongue to touch every curve. I didn't like sucking dick, but I loved sucking his. I would do whatever he asked to please him. That's just how invested I felt in us.

"Daddy, you taste so fucking good," I let him know as I sucked him back into my mouth and bobbed my head up and down a few times. Each time I came up, I would shake my head on the tip.

"Do I?" He groaned.

Instead of answering him with words, I slurped on his dick just to let him know how good he actually tasted. I grabbed his dick and did the two-hand twist while I licked the tip.

"Oh, fuck. Get up!" he damned near screamed. I got up, laughing. "You always do that shit. Almost make a nigga bust fast. Now, bring that ass here." He smirked.

I went to him, and he kissed me passionately.

Kash slowly slid inside me while grabbing the shower head off its rightful place. The smile he gave let me know I was in for a treat.

"Baby, you hear that?" I asked.

Kasha stepped out of the shower and walked over to the bathroom door.

Grabbing a towel, I wrapped it around my body and went behind him. When he walked into the bedroom and shut the door, I wanted to ask what he was doing.

Grabbing me by the waist, he kissed my lips. "Listen, don't come out of this room, no matter what you hear. Hide some-where and call Von but stay quiet. Don't even say anything. He gon' know something is wrong," he whispered as he grabbed his gun and eased out the door.

He never even put any clothes on, so I didn't know what he was going to do butt ass naked with a gun. It was the wrong time to think of him as sexy, but the way he was so ready to protect me let me know how deeply he cared for me.

Looking around the room, I couldn't find anywhere to hide. All the places I thought of were dumb, and I knew for damn sure I wasn't getting under the bed. Dialing Von's number, I stayed quiet until I heard him say hello.

"I think someone is in here. Kash went to check," I whispered.

The moment I said that, I heard a big crash. I wanted to run and see what was going on, but I didn't move. I could hear Von saying he was on his way, but that didn't help me. I looked around the room and still couldn't think of anywhere to hide. Running to the door, I locked it. I could hear people talking and more things being tossed around.

"We ain't come for no money, nigga. This shit is personal," I heard.

"Fuck you mean it's personal? I don't know you niggas. The only thing y'all could want from me is money," Kash snapped back.

"Nigga, you killed my sister," I heard someone yell before shots rang out.

Instead of staying quiet, my dumb ass screamed. I heard footsteps, and the closer they got, the more scared I became. I looked for something around the room to help me but found nothing. Everything in the room would only be good for one swing, and that was it. The room door came crashing down, and two masked people stepped in.

"I should have known this bitch would be here." I recognized the voice all too well.

"Capri? I thought he was your brother," I said and ran toward the other side of the room.

Knowing they would follow, I knocked the guy over his head and darted past Capri.

When I got down the stairs and saw Kash laid out on the floor, I stopped and let out a gut-wrenching scream.

"Bitch, shut up!" she said.

Capri hit me over the head, and everything faded to black.

CHAPTER THREE

AMARIE

When I opened my eyes, the pounding in my head made me groan. The throbbing pain was like a beating in my head that happened over and over again. Leaning back against the wall, I looked around at my surroundings. I could tell just by the smell of mold or mildew that I was in somebody's basement.

I didn't have to think too much to know that I had messed up. All I could think of was how I had gotten myself there by simply not following directions. My mind quickly wandered to Kasha and if he was okay. Images of him lying on the ground surrounded by blood invaded my thoughts. He looked dead, and that's what scared me the most. I was no help to him, and I damn sure was no help to myself. If anything, now was the time for me to focus on the street knowledge that I did have. Trying to think hard about what to do, I came up empty since all I could think of was Kash and if he was really dead. I wanted this to all be a dream and for his friend to not have done him like that.

"Now ain't the time to be trying to dwell on some shit that already happened," I told myself aloud.

I needed to figure a way out of there, so I could help him. The entire time I sat and thought about Kash, my auntie's voice played in my head.

"Stop trying to help everyone when you're in the position of needing to help yourself. Girl, help yourself first, and that's when you can offer some help to others. You ain't much help if you need help."

This was a moment when I really needed her to say that to me. My ass was so focused on getting to Kash and helping him because he had been helping me so much that I forgot to help myself first. As I stood, the ache in my head grew, and it felt like it was trying to push through my eyes. Doing my best to ignore the pain, I took slow and quiet steps toward the staircase that led to a closed door. Trying my luck, I twisted the knob, and since it wasn't locked, I wanted to open it. But hearing the voices on the other side of the door made me stand there and just listen.

"You heard any word on the nigga yet? I mean, the bitch should be waking up soon. Her ass been down there knocked out for a few hours now. How hard you hit the bitch upside her head, Pri?" I heard someone ask.

"Shit, I don't know. And I ain't heard nothing yet. Knowing his parents, they have him somewhere private, or they did what they could to not let word spread. Von texted me, but I'm gon' pull up and act as if I was sleep and didn't see the text and shit until now. Everybody knows I'm a heavy sleeper," Capri replied.

After tiptoeing down the stairs, I sat back down just as the door opened. I watched silently as the two walked down. Capri looked like her usual pretty self, but instead of her hair being braided, it was in a back bun. The smile on her face made me angry. There was nothing to smile about, not to me, anyway.

"What's up, beautiful?" Capri causally spoke like she didn't have me abducted and in somebody's basement.

"Girl, fuck you. Kash is supposed to be your friend, your bro, and you do him how you did him?" I shouted.

I wanted to get up and smack the smile off her face, but the print of the gun on her waist kept me from doing so. The small smirk on the guy's face made my frown deepen.

"Oh, little ma is a feisty one, huh?" he asked her, and she shrugged.

"I ain't never seen her act like this, so it's surprising. I'm trying to be nice to you. I know I busted yo' shit, and that's why I wrapped your head up. You got a small gash and a little knot, but that's all. On some real shit, Amarie, you weren't supposed to get hurt in all this. It was strictly meant for Kash, but you were just there. Usually, I leave no witnesses. However, I fucks with who I fucks with, and I don't want to hurt her," Capri explained.

I looked at her and decided not to say anything. If the bitch wanted to play nice because of my cousin, that's what we would do. I needed to get out of there, and she hadn't spoken on that.

"Listen, can you just let me go? I need to go home." I wanted to beg, but I refused.

If they were going to kill me, I didn't want to go out begging. Truth was, I wanted revenge, and I hadn't even made it out of there yet.

"It ain't that simple, baby. You must don't know who you have as a man and what he and his family are capable of. Von is about to paint the city red behind him, and I'm going to help. I can't do that if I let you free, simply because you will tell him who did this. You can sit here and say, 'I'll take this to the grave' and all those things you can think to say, but I ain't trying to hear that shit. Thats your man, so you gon' tell. Plus, you ain't street, and you look like you would snitch as soon as you can." She rolled her eyes.

"This is why I said kill the bitch," the guy said.

"You lost your mind, bro. If this nigga alive, and we kill her, Kash gon' go bat shit crazy. Nobody gon' be able to tell him nothing. He not only has a team to back him, but he is the one with the money, and he'd be willing to pay anything to find out what happened to her. He's gon' be mad about getting caught lacking, but he's gon' make shit shake really bad behind her."

Hearing her speak on Kash and how he felt about me made me smile on the inside. I knew I needed to play this smart because it was clear they didn't have a plan.

"Who gives a fuck what he may do? That nigga may die too, and that's what we want. He killed my fucking sister and made my mom cry. I'm trying to make every muthafucka he loves disappear. How you don't feel like that when she was your sister too?"

"Yeah, she was my sister, which is why I helped you. But if you want to be honest, he was more of my family than she was. Those people accepted me for me, allowed me to be who I truly am, and that's what's fucking me up," she snapped before walking off.

"She may not kill you, but I'm going to do you just like I did Kash bitch ass," he barked at me before storming back up the stairs and slamming the door.

In that moment, I knew that I would have to play off Capri's feelings and hope she never left me alone with that man. Sitting back against the wall, I felt defeated. I was back at square one and was over it. After a few minutes, I stood, walked up the stairs, and lightly knocked on the door. My throat was scratchy, and I badly needed something to drink.

"What's up, ma?" Capri opened the door with a look of defeat on her face.

"Can I get something to drink?" I asked.

Capri turned and grabbed a bottle of water, but the guy knocked it out of her hand.

"Let the bitch die of dehydration," he yelled, and she pushed him back.

"Stop fucking playing with me, nigga! I ain't the same little girl you used to pick on." She pushed him again.

While they yelled back and forth at each other, I took the time to look around. The basement door was in the kitchen. There wasn't a back door, and the way the kitchen was set up, I couldn't see the front door.

"Bitch, I don't give a fuck who you think you are. You are not the nigga you always thought you were. Your dick comes off, and you got a pussy, making you a bitch. I'll still beat your ass like I used to. Now, you either in or you ain't, but the bitch stays here, and she's dying!" he yelled.

Capri swung on him, punching him in the face. He looked at her with a stunned expression. While the two of them fought, I eased against the wall into the kitchen, trying my best not to make any noise that would cause them to stop fighting and grab me. Capri held the back of the guy's shirt and was swinging wildly with the other hand.

Once I made it to the kitchen opening, I hauled ass to the front door. After unlocking it, I pulled it open, only for the dumb ass alarm to sound off.

Front door

Hearing the tussling stop, I rushed down the stairs, hoping someone was outside. Not knowing where I was and only seeing a house about five hundred feet away, I took off running at full speed. I heard footsteps behind me and a whole lot of cursing.

"Stop, or I'm going to shoot you," I heard the guy yell, which made me run faster.

It felt like I was being chased by cops the way he was yelling that he would shoot me. I ran up the stairs to the neighbor's porch and started banging on the door.

"Help, please."

An older lady came to the door and raised one of her eyebrows at me. She looked behind me and quickly slammed the door shut. Turning around, I moved right into a hand around my throat.

"See, bitch, now you have to get tied the fuck up like I said in the first place. You in my area, and these people know not to fuck with me or say shit." He snatched me up.

Using all my strength, I tried to push him off me, but it didn't work. He easily lifted me off my feet, and I started to punch him anywhere my fists would land. There was no way he would get me back into the house that easily. Hell, someone was going to say they saw me, even if it wasn't the old bitch who was scared to help me.

"Oh, you a pretty strong bitch. You better hope I don't take this pussy and knock you the fuck out too, or I might like it and make you my bitch. You gon' bow down to me, though," he barked as he kept walking with me.

"You ain't getting shit. You might as well kill me. I ain't making shit easy for you."

I kicked my feet in hopes that he would drop me and I could run again, but his big ass didn't seem fazed. Once he got to the stairs, I bit him on top of his head as hard as I could. In my mind, I figured if I fell, I could grab the railing to help me.

"Stupid bitch! Let me go!" he screamed out in pain, but I wasn't letting up.

I locked down harder like a pit bull and began to shake. His screams grew louder, and eventually, it sounded like he wanted to cry. I was gon' make him think twice about taking any pussy from me because if he tried, I would bite a chunk out of his ass.

Out of nowhere, I felt someone pulling me, making me bite down harder.

"Let go, Amarie, damn," Capri lowly said, but I didn't give a damn.

If I had two mouths, I would have bitten her ass too.

The guy started punching me in the face. He delivered one punch to my eye that made me see a light flash, and I quickly let go. At that point, he swung me so quickly and hard off him that I didn't have time to grab the railing. My back hit the step, causing a wave of pain to shoot through my body. He then pulled his gun from his waist and aimed it at me.

Hearing the boom and feeling Capri's body fall on top of mine had me screaming for dear life.

"You next, bitch. Soon as I'm done with you," he said while dragging me by my hair into the house.

CHAPTER FOUR

VON

Watching all of those people come and go in the hospital was crazy to me. It had been two days, and my brother was still out of it. I wanted niggas' heads behind this, but what had me the most confused was Amarie. It was like she vanished without a trace, and the only people I knew who could reach her couldn't.

"So, you ever leave this room?" the nurse asked when she walked in. She was the same nurse from the night before.

I thought for a second before I responded.

"Yeah, I do. Do you ever just do your fucking job?" I responded.

Each time she came in, she made small talk with me like I wanted to talk. I didn't even want to be in there, but my boy's mom was having a hard time coming up to the hospital and seeing her son in that condition, which I understood. My ears needed to be to the streets, and since they couldn't, I had people out there for me. What got me was the fact that everyone was coming up with a bunch of nothing. Shit wasn't adding up.

I knew my boy needed me there, but without my presence in the streets and bodies not dropping, no one was going to speak. I needed to let people know I was coming.

"That's a part of my job. You are here, so I speak to you. It would be rude if I just walked in here, did whatever, and walked out," she sassed.

"I like shit that way. Just come in and do what you have to unless you can offer me some information on my brother, which you haven't done. Shit, I hear his heart beating, but you keep checking the shit like you can't hear it, too," I spat.

I didn't need her thinking for a second that I saw anything in her other than what she was. I needed my brother to get better, and that was part of her job. Now, had I seen her outside of this, and circumstances were different, I may have let her thirsty ass suck my dick, but we weren't on that.

"I'm sorry. I just like what I see and was really just trying to make small talk while doing my job. I didn't mean to make you upset."

I watched as she did whatever she needed to do and then quietly walked out with her head down. Kash's mom walked in just in time because I couldn't take this quiet shit no more, and I needed to talk to someone I knew.

"Hey, did they say anything? Has he made any attempts to move or wake up?"

"Nah, same stuff. Ma, look, I'm gon' be completely honest with you. I'm gon' pay somebody to sit up here. I really can't do this shit. I need to be out in them streets getting answers and doing what I need to do behind my brother."

I was sure she knew what I was saying without me saying it. I needed to go outside and cause havoc. Everyone should have known I was coming and started to prepare themselves. Anyone we had beef with in the past, or anyone I thought had a problem or ever looked at my boy funny, was a walking target to me.

"Javon, now you know I don't want you to go out there and get yourself in trouble. However, I know you not gon' listen, so please be careful. I love you, son." She pulled me into a hug and kissed my cheek.

Ma was right. Listening had never been one of my strong points. I heard what I wanted, and I did what I wanted my entire life, which was why my parents dealt with me how they did. I was one of those kids who had great parents and still just did what the fuck I wanted, and they couldn't do shit about it. Even still, they supported me until I was grown.

"I got you. I love you too, lady."

I left that hospital room with one thing on my mind. Kill or be killed. Whichever happened to me, I knew it was all for a good cause. My brother would have moved the same way about me.

Taking the elevator to the parking garage, I paid my ticket before going to my car. Once in my car, I let the tears fall that I had been holding in. I had to be strong while I was in that hospital, watching my brother fight for his life. He wasn't even really into any street shit, which made me even madder because I was always on the streets. If niggas wanted me, I was never hard to find. I also knew somebody had to be watching to even be able to get to his house and get inside. Not too many knew where he laid his head. I was more the type to have bitches in and out of my crib, which was why this wasn't adding up.

If I found out Amarie or her family had something to do with this, Kash would have to be mad at me because the bitch and anybody connected to her would really end up in a bad situation. I was going to kill everyone in her family, from baby to eighty.

Driving down Market Street, I went straight to my block. Baltimore Ave was popping like it usually was on a nice day, and I loved it. However, I wasn't able to show that shit because I was ready to shoot everybody for cooking out while my boy was laid up half dead. Grabbing my gun, I cocked it, ready to let off a few shots in the air to get my crew's attention. However, risking the lives of the kids or one of the females was against everything I stood for. Now, I would kill a bitch if I had to, but it was never my first resort. I did have some manners, although there were very few of them.

Tucking my gun, I jumped out of my car, stormed over to the speaker that was blasting music, and knocked that bitch over. Once the music stopped, everyone looked around, and a few people yelled that whoever was playing the music was fucking up.

"I need all my niggas at the spot now. I don't give a damn what you got going on. If you ain't there in ten minutes, I'm knocking heads off. So, send out y'all messages and whatever else."

I walked down the street and into the house that sat between two apartment complexes. To outsiders, the house looked worn down and old. It had two doors, making it look like an apartment building, and it was. However, upstairs was where my work was cooked up, and downstairs through the back door, was where we took it out. The house had so many entrances and exits that no one would never suspect anything was going on unless they were involved. The basement was where I held meetings. It was soundproof, and a lot of disloyal niggas lost their lives down there too.

I sat on the edge of the sofa while members filed in. I guess they knew I wasn't playing because before I knew it, everyone was there except two people, Capri and Boogie.

"Anybody heard from Capri or Boogie?" I asked, and a lot of nos filled the air.

Shooting Capri a text, I made a mental note to swing by her house later to see what the fuck was up with her. She had days when she went missing, but we always were able to get in contact with her.

"Y'all already know what we here for. I'm not sleeping until bodies drop behind mine. Now, it clearly seems like you niggas wasn't listening for no information since y'all was out here having a damn good time. Kash may not have a hand in moving any of this work, nor the drug shit. However, he is just as much a part of this team as I am. Without him, none of us would be in the position to eat like we do. So, when something happens to him, I need y'all moving like y'all mama in trouble. Now, I want something. I need something to go on, and I want it today," I stated just as Boogie walked through the door.

"My bad, Von. I was deep in some pussy." He smiled like shit was funny. Picking my gun up off the couch, I sent a shot to his head, making his body drop.

Jace, who was standing next to him, jumped so hard that it made me laugh.

"Nigga, you good?" Jace asked.

"You're questioning me? 'Cause, this clip got a good nineteen more shots, and one could be for you. I ask the questions. Ain't nobody selling shit until I get something. Shut all this shit down. I catch you niggas partying and all that, I'm sending y'all up to the higher power. If you don't like it, speak up now, 'cause I'm on whatever," I spat.

When nobody said anything, I made the call for all my blocks to be shut down. Smokers wasn't smoking, and niggas wasn't making no money. If I caught wind of some shit being served without my say so, I would murk the person serving and the one being served.

Standing up, I walked out, slamming the door behind me. I jumped in my car and drove fifteen minutes to Capri's house. Leaving my car on, I got out and walked up to her front door. Just like usual, the damn door was unlocked. When I walked in, there was no sign of her ass. Everything was left just like it was the last time I met her over there, down to the cereal bowl I left on the counter.

Now, Capri was one of those super clean people, so that threw me off. As I walked through the house, I prepared myself to find some shit I didn't want to see since the last house I went into that was this quiet, I found Kash's ass.

A slight weight lifted off my shoulders when I didn't see her. If she wasn't there, more than likely, she was with Nakari, who was probably at home. Walking out, I locked the door and jogged to my car. The amount of shit I didn't know was getting me more heated by the minute.

Putting my car in drive, I did double the speed limit to Nakari's house. When I pulled up, I saw Natalia's car parked in the driveway behind Nakari's car. I threw my shit in park, hopped out, and walked the short path to her front door. I banged on it like I was the police.

Natalia swung the door open, gun in hand, with a deep frown on her face. The moment we locked eyes, her frown seemed to deepen. Even with the unpleasant expression, her beauty almost made me forget what I was there for. Natalia was pretty as hell to me, and her nasty attitude that should have made me want to smack her ass only made me like her that much more. Her curvy body attracted me like a motherfucker. She always had on some booty shorts, and I loved how her ass ate them up. Natalia was the type to stay dressed no matter the occasion. Shit, I had slept with her a few times, and she always had on silk pajamas with slippers to match.

"Why the fuck are you banging on my sister's door like that?" she snapped.

"Where Capri ass? She here? Your sister got her locked in the room, munching on her box?" I brushed past her, letting myself in.

"No, I don't. I ain't talked to her in about two days. She left here saying she had something important to do, and I ain't heard from her since." Nakari sipped her juice while looking through her phone.

"Aye, Tali, didn't you say all y'all had that Find My iPhone shit? Did y'all try searching Amarie?" I asked them.

"Yeah. Her phone pings at Kash's house," Natalia said.

"What about her AirPods? Watch? Something," I asked.

When they looked at each other, I knew then that they hadn't checked that.

"Look, at this point, I don't have Capri, and I'm gon' need some help with this shit. At least if y'all don't want me to think y'all up to something and then get to killing y'all off one at a time." I smirked at them but meant every word I said.

CHAPTER FIVE

NAKARI

Natalia handed me the phone, and I hesitated for a minute before going through the messages. Nothing seemed off about the last text either of us got from Amarie. She was just about to enjoy some alone time with her man. What did get me was the voice message from Von that he had sent her about how he was upset that the streets weren't talking too much. I could hear the hurt and sincerity in his voice. He wanted whoever was behind this dead, even if it came down to it being the woman he had grown accustomed to having in his bed.

I would've thought by now that he had a soft spot for Natalia, but his ass was on some fuck the world type shit. I could understand why he felt like that because I wanted to know what was going on with Capri. Pulling up Find My iPhone, I searched Amarie's watch, which was last at Kash's house, along with her phone. Tapping on her AirPods, one showed at Kash's house while the other was somewhere else. When I zoomed in on it, I saw that it was in Drexel Hill and knew I may have found something. Amarie's ass didn't know anyone in Drexel Hill.

"Hey, look, her AirPod is in Drexel Hill," I said aloud, showing Natalia.

"Who the fuck lives in Drexel Hill?" Natalia asked while Von snatched the phone from my hand.

He did something before tossing my phone on the counter and walking out. I checked my phone to make sure it wasn't broken and then looked at the screen. He had enlarged the map to street level, and I was sure he was on his way there.

"Should we call the police?" I asked Natalia.

"Fuck no. That's the last thing we should do. Von would probably go to jail, and that's the best chance we got at finding out what's really going on. Do you think Capri is missing or just don't want to be bothered with the world?" Natalia asked.

"I don't know. I do know we can't just sit around and do nothing. I mean, we can't go to the police, but what can we do? We got enough street in us to know we can make something happen."

"Girl, you know damn well we not like that. We would have to call on Mommy, and she's going to lose her shit. For one, we didn't tell her right away, and for two, you know how she feels about Amarie. I mean, we have our guns, but we can't use them because it will come back to us. This is past fighting over boys or because we're cute. This also ain't bagging up little bags of weed and selling them." Natalia briefly closed her eyes and took a deep breath, like she was thinking of what to say next.

"So, what do you suggest? We get some dirty guns and start shooting shit up too?" I asked.

I was always down to shoot my gun. Hell, I was so good at it that I knew I could bust a few heads wide open.

"Nakari, I'm serious. We ain't busting no heads." Natalia mugged me.

"Shit, well, sitting here talking ain't done shit for us but let time pass us by."

"So, what the fuck are we doing?" She asked the same question, and it was getting on my nerves.

"We call Mommy. That's all we can do. She gon' snap, but at least we'll let her know. Von is out here moving on his own, and I really feel like maybe Capri has something to do with this. Think about it, the same night she got something important to do is the night this shit happens, and now nobody can find her or Amarie. That's too coincidental. She would also be able to get into Kash's house with ease." I said what had been on my mind.

"Oh shit, you really think Capri would do some shit like that, though? Like, you really think she would try to kill Kash?" Natalia asked.

It made sense to me, or maybe I had watched too many TV shows.

DeJuan wasn't even a candidate to pull some shit like that. His family would have had to hire someone, and with the debt they were going into, I was sure they didn't have the money to do so. Plus, most people knew that if they did something to Kash, Von would come for them. DeJuan's family wasn't the type to want street problems; they would gracefully bow out.

"What about her mom? Auntie wants money, and that's a way to get it," Natalia threw out.

"Yeah, again, though. It's a lot to come with it. Why would she sue her and then kidnap her? That would raise a flag and point fingers at Auntie. I say we go to the cops or call Mommy. Either way, we have to get help because we need it. The street bitches we think we are, we are not."

Of course, we had some ratchet in us. Watching our mom

fight, and all the other things gave us street cred, but we didn't really have a street bone in our bodies. We were the smart girls who were cool with everyone and fit in. We snuck to parties and hung with a few drug dealers, but that was it. People thought we knew more about the streets than we did, and this situation alone showed our hand. We weren't like that, and we probably never would be. That didn't mean we couldn't get what we needed to be done, though. With one phone call to my moms, she would have her ex look into it, and things would get done.

"Hey, Siri, call Mother Bear," I called out.

In seconds, the phone rang.

"What's up, baby girl?" My mom answered the phone.

"Ma, can you call Mr. Ray and come to my house? Natalia and I are here, and we need y'all," I said, and my mom hung up.

That lady never liked to discuss things over the phone. My mom was one of those people who knew everybody and swore her phone was tapped. Had I gone into detail, she probably would have popped me in the mouth when she saw me.

Fifteen minutes went by with us sitting at the table, writing down names and why they would be a suspect. My mom and Mr. Ray walked in, and of course, my mom put an extra switch into her walk.

"What's up?" she asked, getting straight to it.

Natalia and I looked at each other, wondering who was gon' tell her because I damn sure didn't want to be the one.

"I know damn well y'all ain't called me and him over here to watch y'all hang y'all heads. What's going on? And tell me right now."

When that lady put bass in her voice, I still got scared like I was still a kid.

"We can't find Amarie. She was with Kash, who was shot

two nights ago," I said as quickly as the good lord would allow me to get it out.

"She what?" my mom said, looking at me.

"Mom, you heard me," I whispered.

"And you just now telling her? I heard about that Kash shit but ain't get no details on it because I didn't know you young ladies were attached to them little niggas. Kash a good dude. Hell, I'm surprised Von ass ain't paint the city red yet," Mr. Ray said.

"He just left here, and in his mind, maybe Amarie had something to do with it. Only because he can't find her, and we ain't even attempt to call the police." Natalia spoke for the first time since they walked through the door.

"That's not good. Von is one of those kill you first, and think about if he made the wrong move after. If he hasn't killed anyone yet about this, I'm sure he will soon start, and that may include some of y'all family members if he doesn't start getting answers. Now, I'm gon' reach out to him and see where his head's at." Mr. Ray pulled his phone out and dialed a number.

A few seconds later, he set his phone down and looked around. He stood, walked to the window, and looked out.

"Aye, what color is your neighbor's car?"

"Huh?" I was taken aback by his question.

"Answer the damn question. I'm trying to be quiet over here and figure my damn words out. What the fuck possessed you two not to tell me the moment shit happened? Y'all ain't like that. The closest y'all would have gotten to this was sitting here making notes of what y'all thought could have happened. Y'all could have made that phone call to me, and we could have been got Amarie back. I'm not angry at all at you two for trying to handle shit. I'm upset because you know we could have had people in the streets making shit happen." My mom went from an angry parent to a soothing one.

"We know we fucked up, which made us wait even longer to call you. Now her AirPod pinged at some house in Drexel. Von was here, and he left. I think he went there to check it out," I told them.

"What's the location on that? I'm gon' have a few of my people check that out. I hear Kash isn't doing too well. Hopefully, it's different for Amarie. Whatever y'all do, don't call the cops. Getting them involved will only make shit more complicated. I mean, of course, they know about Kash being shot. However, placing Amarie at the scene will have her as a suspect rather than a missing person." Mr. Ray told us something that we suspected and feared.

We all knew Amarie wasn't like that. Hell, she wasn't even really into confrontation. However, just because we knew her didn't mean anyone else did, and the cops would have to do their job and cross off all leads.

"So, what do we do?" I asked.

I had done enough sitting pretty. It was time to get dirty.

"Nothing. I know y'all want to help, but y'all can possibly make matters worse by stepping into it. For one, you all wouldn't know what to do, and that will only make y'all walking targets. Now, again, I ask what color is your neighbor's car?"

"It's a gold Nissan. Her boyfriend's car is a white Charger with mirror tint," I answered.

"Somebody is watching y'all. Now, I'm sure if you said Von just left, it's his people, meaning he may want to kill y'all. All of you, and I'm not gon' say he wrong because if it was me, I'd be on the same type of time. Now, what I'm gon' do is go speak to his people and have them reach out to him. I'm gon' let him know to stand back, and if he doesn't, we will have a problem, which will create a big war if need be. Before I do that, is there anything I need to know? Like, is there a possibility Amarie or y'all could have anything to do with this? Know that I'm standing behind y'all, but I'm not trying to walk into this blindfolded."

Mr. Ray was calm and soft-spoken. He'd always had that demeanor. He and my mom were together for years until his baby mother came around with their son. My mom couldn't take him having a child on her, so she left. I had never seen him raise his voice, not even when he was visibly upset. I even remember going to his son's funeral with my mom. Of course, we sat front row with the family, and even then, he didn't raise his voice nor cry.

"No," we said in unison.

Mr. Ray nodded before picking his phone back up. I let out a breath because now I felt like we were making something happen, even if we weren't the ones doing it ourselves. However, the look my mother had on her face had me scared to death. She wasn't at ease, and when her ass wasn't at ease, no one had a good day.

CHAPTER SIX
VON

The city was quiet and making me grow impatient as hell. Whoever was behind this had made a bold move. I took a pull from the blunt that I had pre-rolled and deeply inhaled it. My car was now cut off, and thanks to the deep tints on my windows, no one would be able to tell I was in it. I was parked at the top of the block where Amarie's AirPods had shown. So far, there was no sign of her. I was moving alone because I felt like I couldn't trust anyone.

Mr. Ray had called my phone, which I declined to answer. He was one of the old heads who used to be heavy in the streets a few years ago. He took a few bullets, and his kid was killed, which ultimately made him sit his ass down and come out the game. I felt for him, but at the same time, I was kind of happy since that gave my crew more range to sell drugs and not cause us any beef.

Mr. Ray was one of those men whose team was still loyal to him, so he could move how he wanted and not be bothered. Hell, the person who shot him was killed the next day, and in the following days, their family started dropping, and now the home that used to belong to the family was empty. Mr. Ray had kept it standing. He said it was to remind people not to fuck with him. I didn't really see Amarie making that move, but I couldn't put shit past anyone.

It felt like hours had gone by before I watched a guy leave one of the houses. He looked around before hopping into a car similar to Capri's. He speed off, and a few minutes later, he returned with some Chinese food. He had on one of those dumb ass ski masks that everyone was wearing, so I couldn't really make out his face. I watched as he stood on the steps, talking on his phone. He seemed to be in a heated argument.

Seconds later, an older lady walked out of the house next door and the two started talking. Needing to hear what was being said, I pressed the button on my car to turn it on just long enough to crack my window. I still couldn't hear them, so I said fuck it and got out the car, then walked over. They were so into the conversation that they didn't see me coming.

"That was my girlfriend, Ma. We were into it, and she always does that dramatic shit like I'm trying to hurt her," he explained.

"Excuse me, but have either of you seen some AirPods around here? I went for a jog this morning and dropped mine. I'm new in this area," I smoothly lied.

Looking at the guy, something was familiar about him. I didn't know him, but I felt like I had seen him somewhere. Hell, he looked like somebody I knew. From the way he was frowning at me, I knew he felt the same.

"Nah, we ain't see shit," he barked.

"Actually, I did. It was on your steps when that girl was running. I don't know if it was an AirPod, but it looked like a headphone."

Dude looked at the old lady like he wanted to kill her.

Instead of saying anything, I pulled my hand from my

pocket and motioned with my gun for them to walk up the stairs. The front door of the house was wide open, and while I wanted to kill them both right where they stood, I knew where I was.

The old lady shot daggers at me, and I didn't care. On a normal day, I wouldn't pull a gun on an old lady, but this old bitch was dying today. When this nigga attempted to go the other way, I pulled my other gun and placed it on the back of his head.

"Please don't make me bust your head in front of this old lady," I spoke through clenched teeth.

"Oh, lord, help me. This man been giving me hell since his mother left him this house. I done watched him kill that girl after I didn't open my door for him. Lord bless our souls. Cover us and touch this man with this gun."

"Come on now, ma'am. I don't want to interrupt a prayer because my mom would beat me for that. But the Lord ain't about to help you or this nigga if you don't shut the fuck up and tell me what I need to know." Kicking the door shut behind me, I waited for one of them to start speaking.

"I ain't killed nobody. This bitch tripping."

"You a darn lie! Ever since Rosella left you that damn house, you been doing whatever. I told her you were crazy and needed to be in therapy. Now that girl was running, and she banged on my door for help. That's what you were just out there explaining. She's your girlfriend. Rosella always thought you would get better, but I knew that was a lie. Then, you killed that poor girl. I watched you do it!" the old lady yelled, and I had enough of her.

Making sure the silencer was on my gun, I asked God to really forgive me for this one. I knew I was going straight to hell whenever it was my time, yet this would be the one that reserved my spot. I raised my gun and almost burst out laughing when this lady started shouting and praying like she had the Holy Ghost. I watched her for a second before I knocked her soul out and whatever else was in her.

"One down, one to go. Now, it seems you got some answers to my questions," I said while we sat in this lady's house.

I shot my guys a message to come over. I needed all this shit cleaned up, and if the old lady had cameras, I needed it to be like they never existed. For the right price, it would get done.

"I don't have shit. If you gon' kill me, kill me. You still gon' wonder who sent me." He laughed.

"I mean, I could just kill you like you want me to, but what fucking fun would that be? I'm thinking I'm gon' get my answers one by one, but I'm gon' do some shit to you each time. You should have known that I was gon' come for you. Even if it took me the rest of my life to find you, I would have." I laughed.

"You doing all this behind a nigga? Man, let me find out y'all fucking." He laughed back.

"The ignorance is real, and I respect your hand right now. You're standing tall but watch how I break your ass down. And about the 'I'm gon' always wonder who sent you' comment, we gon' get back to that later. Every single piece of information I want to know, you gon' tell me. And every nigga I need to die behind my brother gon' die. I'll meet you in hell and kill you again," I let him know.

Hearing the signature tap, I let my crew in. Instead of going back to my car, I walked to the house that I saw dude come out of. Since I didn't feel like climbing a gate or anything, I picked the lock on the front door, which sounded off the alarm system to let whoever was there know the front door was open.

Looking around, the first thing I noticed was a large trail of blood. I sucked in a deep breath, knowing I would have to be the one to break the bad news to everyone. Walking deeper into the house, my mouth dropped when I saw Capri on the floor with a hole in her head. Of course, I wanted to cry for her, but the thug in me wouldn't allow it, especially when I saw Amarie. Running over to her, I ripped off the tape from her mouth and untied her hands. I expected her to cry, but a look of defeat was the only thing covering her face.

"Kash? He good?" she asked.

"I don't know. Look, my day has been long. He's in the hospital, and he hasn't woken up yet, but he will. I need to know what the fuck happened," I said, looking over at Capri.

"She helped him. Her brother. He killed her because she didn't really want to kill Kash. She got to talking about how y'all accepted her. However, she was the one who brought him into the house, so it's all confusing to me. I guess she'll never get to explain why she helped," Amarie said.

That shit threw me for a loop because Capri was one of us. She was part of the team, so why did she participate in something that would cause harm to one of us. I knew she had family, but she never spoke on them, simply because they didn't agree with who she was, and it didn't fit into their holy background. I remember her saying she had a brother. He was older than her by a few years, but she did her best to stay from around them. I wondered what changed her mind. What made her feel like she needed to help him? And as I stared into her eyes that were wide open, I knew I would forever have those questions.

As much as I wanted to be mad at Capri, I couldn't. Shit, being mad wouldn't change shit, and it eased my mind that I didn't have to kill her. Without a second thought, if she was alive, I would have left her in the same state she was in now. Many times, I would find myself going back and forth with decisions like now. I wanted to kill this man and just deal with whatever came. However, I also wanted to torture him until Kash woke up, and then let him decide his fate.

"Come on. Let's get you home." I walked Amerie out to my car.

I let her climb in before I walked over to my guys. To the naked eye, it looked like pest control was outside, when in actuality, we were cleaning everything that could have possibly indicated that I was ever there. Pulling my gun from my hip, I wiped it clean.

"Terrell, is it? Here, hold this." I held out the gun without the clip in it.

When he refused to take it, I grabbed the blender off the counter and plugged it up. I turned it on and held it over his head. He quickly grabbed the gun, and I let him hold it while I tossed the blender into the trash can that my guys had brought. With a glove covered hand, I made sure to tell my guys to place the clip back in and take it next door to his house.

I was going to make sure someone notified the police, so the old lady could have a proper burial. Meanwhile, Capri's ass would rot until someone found her, which would also be where they find the gun that killed the old bitch, and case closed.

CHAPTER SEVEN

AMARIE

"One more dumb thing, and I'm going to kill you. Now, let's try and make you at ease to help this run smoother. I'm Terrell. Capri and I are half siblings. Your boyfriend killed my sister a while back. I've been plotting to kill him for a while now and couldn't find the right time. Capri owed me some money for a case I took for her, and since she waited so long to pay me, I did the only thing I could think of. I let her know she had to pay me, or I would go to the law and give up all the information I had on them. I knew how Von's business started. Hell, everyone did, but one day I recorded a conversation between all three of them. Capri ain't really want Kash to die, which was why she had to die."

I kept replaying that man's words in my head. He left about an hour ago and hadn't returned. This time, I was tied up to a damn chair in the middle of the living room, staring at Capri's dead body. Hearing the front door, I looked up and waited for him to walk over, only to see Von.

Seeing Von was a breath of fresh air. However, I was scared shitless. I had learned that my abductor's name was Terrell, and that he and Capri were brother and sister. I would be sure to let him know all of that. When he saw Capri, I saw a look in his eyes that I had never seen before. He seemed genuinely hurt. I needed him to see me because I wanted to get the fuck away from there.

Once he finally looked over at me, he snatched the tape off my mouth before untying me. The only thing I could think about was Kash, so when Von told me he wasn't sure if he had woken up, I let my head drop.

Von helped me out of the house, and all I wanted to do was go straight to the hospital to be next to my man. I didn't care about showering or anything, I just wanted to be in his space and know he was okay.

"Von, why are we pulling up to Nakari's house? I need to go to the hospital to see Kash. Could you call whoever is up there and check on him, please?"

"You don't need to go up there like that. Get yourself together and then go," was all he said.

When the car came to a complete stop, Mr. Ray walked outside and came over to the car. He tapped on the window, and Von let it down. By now it was almost completely dark. Seeing Mr. Ray made me smile but not enough to where I felt happy inside. Climbing out of the car, I walked over and gave him a hug.

"Your auntie and cousins are in there worried sick about you. Go see them while I talk to Von." He released me from his arms.

I slowly made my way inside the house and into the living room where everyone quietly sat. My auntie was the first to lay eyes on me. When she did, she jumped up and pulled me into a hug. Nakari and Natalia joined in, and this time, my smile came from within.

"Damn, let me breathe. I missed y'all too." I pushed them off me.

"What happened?" Nakari asked.

"Don't talk about it if you don't want to right now. Just know when the time comes, things will be handled." My auntie gave Nakari a stern look.

"Capri is dead," I announced.

"No, bitch, don't play like that." Nakari backed up just as Von and Mr. Ray walked in.

"I'm not playing. She was there when everything happened," I told her, and Nakari dropped to the floor.

"I knew it! I knew it! You didn't have to kill her, Von. She would have fixed it!" Nakari cried.

"I ain't kill the bitch, but I would have. Anybody who puts my family at risk knows the consequences. They got to die, especially a muthafucka who knows me. She was family to me and Kash. He fed her when she wanted to run away because she couldn't face what we had going on at home. My brother made sure we were in the position to be where we at, so if a muthafucka cross him, it's they ass. They got a better chance of freezing to death while dancing with the devil!" Von yelled.

The veins in his forehead popped out, and I knew he was angry. This wasn't the same Von who looked at Capri dead on the floor. It was like that person had vanished and this person took over.

"He did that because he wanted to. Maybe she had no choice." Nakari tried to take up for Capri, and it made me look over at her in confusion.

Nakari was my favorite cousin, and I prayed to God she just wasn't seeing things clear right now because everything was happening so fast, and I had just broken the news to her that Capri was dead. Everyone quietly stood around, just looking at each other. The only sound in the room was Nakari's sobs. I wanted to be there for her, yet the reason she was crying stopped me. The very same girl she was over there mourning was one of the main reasons that things in my life had taken a turn for the worse.

Hell, my man was fighting for his life because of Capri, and she was supposed to be his best friend. I almost lost my life because of her, and I barely knew the girl. Whatever her reasons were, she now had to take that up with God, but I knew her ass was dirty dancing with the devil.

"If it means anything, we are sorry for your loss, Nakari. It's just that what happened makes it hard for any of us to sympathize with you. Amarie is your best friend. Hell, y'all been tight since I've been around, and that's well over half your lives. Her life could have been taken by the very person you are crying over, which makes it how it is. So, while you're screaming out things, take into consideration why everyone is reacting how they are. I hope you understand that karma seemed to catch up to that girl, and fast. In due time, things will be how they are supposed to be," Mr. Ray spoke, breaking the silence.

Nakari looked at him but didn't say anything. I knew I would have to separate myself from her for a while. I didn't want the way I was feeling to ruin anything between us.

"Von, can you take me to Kash's house, please? I don't want to be here right now," I asked.

"We're having security cameras installed around the outside and the locks and things changed. You should be able to go there tomorrow," he explained.

"Okay. Well, Natalia, can I go by your house, or Auntie, can I stay with you? I can't take this right now, and I really just want to lie down since I clearly can't go be with Kash because of people not understanding the meaning of loyalty," I sarcastically stated.

"Let's not do that because you don't know what the fuck they had going on!" Nakari shouted back at me.

"Girl, y'all was the perfect match. You here acting as if that girl ain't just do what she did. Did you cry about me being gone? Were you this bothered? Cause when I walked in this bitch, you sure as hell didn't look like it. Now, correct me if I'm wrong, but you were just mad at Von a few seconds ago, and he didn't even kill the bitch. Her brother did. After they broke into Kash's house and shot him, she then knocked me over my head and had me in somebody's basement. Yeah, she was acting as if she never wanted that to happen, but if she didn't, she would never have given him the address or came with him. Her main reason behind helping him was because of their sister who Kash supposedly killed. See how even with her family treating her fucked up, she stuck to the family over everything code?" I paused for effect.

"I never said she wasn't wrong, and you simply don't understand. Yes, she got what was coming to her, but that doesn't make it hurt any less. I was sleeping with that girl, confiding in her and experiencing something I never felt before. That's why I'm crying. That's why I'm hurt. You, of all people, should know that family means everything to me. And in some way, she was my family too. Shit, you love Kash, and we all started talking at the same time. I can love her too, right? My love is gone, and my heart hurts. It hurts even more that she did this to you, and I feel bad for her. You know had she not been dead, I would have cut her off. You are my best friend, my little sister, so for you to even question my loyalty to you is crazy." Nakari pulled her hair up into a bun.

I knew she didn't want to fight. Hell, I knew I couldn't beat her, but with the anger I had inside me, I was sure I would beat her ass all over her house in the most disrespectful way. My auntie, who was always the mediator, remained quiet. She watched us closely, and I knew she was waiting to see what we would do. I didn't want to be unprepared, so I wrapped my hair up too, even though I was sore.

"The first person to throw a punch, I'm fucking y'all up. There are ways to talk about shit, and I feel like right now ain't the time. Now, we gon' sit here and soak in our sorrows, but quietly. I'm not scared of either of you two whores, so the first one to throw a slick comment can square up with me. We better than this, and we should be celebrating that you are home, Amarie, because you had us all shook. Nakari, we are here for you, and you can take as much time as you need to grieve. Hell, I'm sure Von and Kash gon' need to grieve too, and if Kash can forgive her, we all can. She's with the Lord now. Her time here was up, and it's nothing we can do to change that. Let her be a lesson to us instead of fighting," Natalia said, shocking the hell out of me.

She was always for a good fight, yet there she was, being a peacemaker.

Everything was happening so fast. I felt like I didn't have time to process anything. It seemed like every five minutes, something else happened. I didn't even think that all those things could happen in twenty-four hours. I was over the entire day, and I wanted to go to bed.

Climbing up the steps, I walked into Nakari's room and found something to wear to bed. I went inside her bathroom and ran a bath since I knew I needed to soak my body. While the bath water ran, I sat on the side of the tub. Everything that happened flooded my memory, yet the sight of both bodies that I saw lying lifeless were the ones that consumed my mind the most. That could have been me had Von not come to my rescue. I owed him so much more than a thank you.

"Thank you, God, for sparing my life," I said as tears fell from my eyes.

I eventually started to sob, and when my auntie came in and held me, it only got worse. She held me tight against her chest and rubbed my head.

"Shit will get better. You just have to let things play out. It'll happen on its own time. Just take time and be happy that you are free, and you have life in your body," my auntie whispered in my ear.

CHAPTER EIGHT

KASH

"Kash, I need you to get up, baby. If you don't, who I'm gon' be able to finish this shit with? You said forever, and I guess your forever wasn't that long, huh?"

Amarie.

"Boy, you know it's crazy because I can't even eat. You always feed me and make sure I'm cool. Who gon' do that? I'm trying to take care of you, and I can't because you won't even get up. I feel like I threw you off your square, you know? Like, had I not been there, you would have been more prepared, more aware."

She paused. I couldn't see her, but I could hear her. I knew her voice all too well, and I knew she was crying. I tried to open my eyes, but it was too hard. I couldn't see anything. Everything was all black.

"My hard ass gon' listen even more now. That's why you got to get up. I miss you, daddy. I love you, Kash. I want to be there next to you, holding your hand, but I can't. I'm sorry." The way she called me daddy stood out.

I wanted to tell her I loved her too, but my mouth seemed glued shut.

I needed to get up, but I didn't know how. I couldn't grab anything because I couldn't see. Using everything I had in me, I felt around for something. I could feel something cold, and I used it to pull myself up while forcing my eyes open.

Once I opened my eyes, I tried to adjust to the bright ass lights. I heard my mom yelling, and I wanted to tell her to shut the fuck up. Her and the beeping sound that probably was embedded in my damn memory. I could hear my dad telling her to calm down as she screamed for the nurse. I heard everybody except the voice I needed to hear. The feeling in my throat was bothering me, and I wanted whatever it was to come out. I couldn't remember too much of what happened to land me in there, but I did remember being in the shower with Amarie and hearing a strange noise. After that, everything was blank.

I sat completely up in the hospital bed, and I was confused like hell. I could remember everyone talking to me. I even remembered Capri; I didn't know if she was there or where I had seen her, but I remembered her.

The doctor came in and started talking. I didn't care what he was saying, I wanted his ass to stop flashing that light in my face. The doctor started to remove the stuff from my throat, letting me know what he was doing with each step.

He pulled the long tube out, and it hurt like a bitch. My mouth was so dry; I didn't want to talk. Looking around the room, I wanted the one person who made me fight to get up. When I didn't see her face, I frowned because I knew I had just heard her. After a few sips of water, I opened my mouth.

"Amarie," I said in a voice that didn't at all sound like mine.

"I'm here, baby. I'm on the phone," she said, and my mom handed it to me.

Amarie had a knot on her forehead and a small gash above

her eye. Closing my eyes, I inhaled deeply as parts of what happened flooded my memory. Seeing her like that was a reminder that I had failed her.

"Baby, I was worried sick about you. I can't wait for you to come home."

"Come," I stated, since it still hurt for me to talk.

I wanted her to come up to the hospital and be with me. I knew for sure they weren't going to let me just go home, so having her there with me was the best thing.

"I can't. Look at me, I'm sure doctors would want to know what happened to me, and I don't have an answer for that. You won't be in there for too long, and I promise to have everything in order when you get home." She looked over at something.

"I'm going to call you back." She hung the phone up, making me wonder what was going on.

"Capri?" I asked Von when he walked into the room.

Knowing her, she wouldn't have missed me being laid up in a hospital bed. She would have teased me. However, I kept picturing her being at the house. Every time I thought of her, I remembered looking up from the floor at her. She mouthed the words, I'm sorry. But sorry for what? What had she done that she was sorry for? That question kept racking my brain. I needed to talk to Von and see if he could fill me in on what happened.

"We gon' chop it up when the time is right," was all he said, and I nodded.

Of course, the nurses and doctors came back into the room and did more tests. I was fine with that until the police came into the room. When they asked everybody to step out, I frowned. There was no way I would cooperate with them.

"Hey, we came to ask you a few questions. Do you recall any of the events from the shooting?" they asked, getting straight to the point.

"No." I didn't even take time to answer them.

I didn't want to talk to them; I didn't need to talk to them.

"Well, if you remember anything, give us a call." They set a card on the table, which I was going to make sure went in the trash.

I was on a straight path, and I was a law-abiding citizen most times. However, I followed the no snitching rule. I wasn't about to tell on anyone and label myself as a rat. That just wasn't in me. I was going to make sure my entire family knew that there would be none of that, especially my mom, who was forever trying to call the police for something.

Everyone walked back into the room, and I kept quiet. I wanted to go home. This bed was uncomfortable, and my wrist was aching. Lifting a little, I took the time to see where I had taken bullets. My chest was wrapped up along with my arms, leg, and foot. Even my hand was covered in gauze.

"How many times?" I asked my mom.

"Seven." She placed her purse on the seat and pointed to each spot. I was covered in holes, and still, no one could take me out.

My mind was set on one thing, and that was revenge, and not for just me. Whoever decided they could hurt my baby, even though I was mad at her, would pay. I knew when I left the hospital, I would have to start the search for a new home and make sure I had that muthafucka covered in cameras around the whole outside. I was never going to take a chance like that again and get caught slipping. That made me wonder who found me and what all had happened.

"I'm going to go. I'll be back in the morning. I'm tired, and your sister is home alone. Probably sneaking another damn boy in," my mom fussed, and that raised an alarm with me.

Emily knew better, and when I got out of the hospital, I would have more than a conversation with her. My mom and dad were too easy on her, and that was exactly why she pulled the shit on them that she pulled.

"Fill me in. What happened?" I asked Von as soon as my parents left.

"You won't believe this shit," Von started.

The more he told me the story, the more I remembered. I could picture everything happening until Amarie screamed.

"That's why Capri said sorry," I said aloud but more to myself,

"What?"

"Capri... I kept picturing her saying sorry. That's why. Where is she now?" I asked, and his face dropped.

"You got her?" I pressed, trying to read between the lines.

"No, her brother did. I have him, though. I'm waiting on you," he told me.

"Good. I want to be the one to speak to him," I said, and he nodded.

"Look, I'd love to sit here with you, but I can't spend another day in this seat. We all told Amarie not to come up here. The cops are lurking around, and we don't need that heat. Your phone is on the nightstand. Call her." Von dapped me up and left.

CHAPTER NINE
AMARIE

Inside the small closet, I had set the final bag on the shelf. Kash was coming home from the hospital, and I was ready to take care of him. It had been a total of eight days since everything had happened, and I hadn't been up to the hospital once.

Kash, of course, was upset about it, and I was too. However, his mother thought it would be best if I got home together for us. I also needed to heal myself. The lump on my forehead had gone down, and the bruises had faded away. The only thing that I had to remind myself of what happened was the small gash that remained on top of my eyebrow.

Kash arriving at any minute meant I had a lot of work to get done. I knew he wasn't really eating like he should have been, so I prepared his favorite meal, which was goulash with cheese and garlic bread. I cleaned the kitchen back up, washed all the bedding, and everything else. The house looked like I had hired someone to clean it. His father had someone clean the blood up off the floor, which was the only help I'd gotten.

"Amarie?" Emily called out.

I walked from the kitchen and watched as Mr. Isaiah helped Kash into the house. Mrs. Kristie followed closely behind them with crutches in her hands.

"Hey, baby." I walked over to him.

Kash looked at me and nodded.

That wasn't the welcome I expected, but I would deal with it. Kash had a big problem with me not coming up to the hospital, and he made it clear every day. Seeing me on Face-Time just wasn't enough for him, and though I got what he was saying, I didn't want to complicate things, nor did I want to speak with the police. While he was in the hospital, I took the time to meet with a few lawyers who were all out of my budget. I needed to draw up some papers to have my mom sign.

"He will get over it. Kash knows that was for the best," Mr. Isaiah told me.

"I'm won't. You were supposed to be there for me. I basically begged you every day to come up there. What was so important that you couldn't for just ten minutes come sit with me? It ain't about what they thought was best. You always let people think for you. I thought it was me and you forever," Kash said, and he genuinely sounded hurt.

"It is and always will be you and me forever. Kash, I honestly thought I was doing the right thing. I wanted to be there. The very first moment Von got me from that place, I asked for you. You can ask him. I wanted to be there for you the best I could. I didn't want the police getting involved and possibly making things even more complicated. I did let everyone decide what I should do, but you can't blame me for trying to listen. The moment I didn't listen to you, I almost got myself killed.

"Kash, I love you, and I'm sorry for not coming up there, but being mad at me won't make you feel any better. I cleaned up and even went ahead and started taking steps for the things with my mom. I made the time we spent apart useful and tried to make you proud. I even heard you say you didn't want to be in this house for much longer, so I started looking for places for you." I grabbed the folder off the table with all the work I had been doing to keep myself busy.

Kash allowed a small smile to form on his face, and I knew he was no longer mad at me. I was going to take care of his every need, even if he decided to still be mad at me. While he was home, he wouldn't need to call on anyone but me.

"I love you too, girl," he let me know, and that was all I needed to hear.

Walking into the kitchen, I quickly fixed Kash some food and took it to him. I sat next to him while he ate, wishing I could be in his skin.

"I can't wait for you to get better, bro. I need to come down here for the summer. I hate Florida," Emily whined as she plopped on the couch across from us.

"You're crazy. I loved every part of Miami. It's amazing there. What's so bad about it?" I asked.

"Everything. Them bitches up there are all stuck up and proper. They think they better than everybody, and then it's the hood rats. Them bitches too ghetto for me, and I thought my cousins was bad. It's like I don't fit in. I'm used to being the girl with everything, like the it girl. This school I'm at, I might as well be broke," she said.

"It's not always about what you have. I probably was in the broke crowd in school, but I made what I had look good. Plus, how you think you broke when you sixteen and carrying a Chanel bag. Hell, I'm grown and still never owned a Chanel bag of my own. You should be thankful for what you have. I remember nights my cousins and I would use the oven to heat the house because the heaters were broken. I'm sure you never had that problem or even had to worry about it. Your friends shouldn't even be your friends for what you have. Y'all should genuinely like each other," I schooled her.

If I knew nothing else, I knew what it was like to have real friends, even if mine were my cousins.

"You make it all seem so simple. Nowadays, it's all about what you have," she replied.

"Even if it is, what don't you have or what can't you ask for? That's what you should focus on. Girl, you literally have the dream life and don't even know it. Hell, I'll call one of the little girls from around my way, and they would die to be in your shoes."

"You're right. I may need to go to this school with a different attitude and try to make friends."

"I also think you owe your parents an apology. I mean, I'm just saying, you low key been giving them hell," I pointed out.

Emily laughed and looked over at her parents, who were leaning against the wall, listening to us. I admired how the entire time, they didn't say anything. They just let me speak to her and allowed her to express how she felt. That was something a lot of parents didn't do.

"Hey, Amarie, can I talk to you for a second?" Mrs. Kristie called out to me.

Standing to my feet, I followed her into the kitchen and took a seat at the counter. She paced the floor for a second before pinching the bridge of her nose and letting out a deep breath.

"Thank you. That girl was driving me to the point of no return, and as a mother, I wasn't sure where I was going wrong. I tried talking to her and taking things, even when I knew I would only give them back. I even went as far as trying to get her therapy when her only problem is simply that she's spoiled. I sometimes feel like I'm failing as a parent, you know, and it's a lot. I really appreciate you talking to her for me because I was ready to knock her damn head off if we're being completely honest here, and I've never raised my hand to my children. Kash and Emily are so different in so many ways. Hell, some days I be ready to let her ass leave and see what the real world is about, but I know that shit would chew my baby up and spit her out," Mrs. Kristie shared with me.

"You're crazy." I laughed. "Sometimes talking doesn't work if you ask my auntie. She would have knocked her out, then gave her what she wanted. We had a lot growing up compared to some people, but not everything. She also made us earn things, and that may help with Emily. You could still give her whatever but make her work for it. Let her know that when she gets out there into the world, nothing will just be given to her because of who her parents are. She will have to work for it, and the things you work for, you cherish more. That's just a suggestion. You don't have to actually do that," I said.

I didn't even know how I was giving advice when my life was in shambles. I just knew that growing up, I watched how my cousins swore up and down they deserved everything we had, while I didn't care if we went to Payless to get shoes; I was just happy to get some.

"You're a good girl. I hope my son sees that in you and makes you a part of this family." Kash's mom winked at me before walking off.

I sat there for a second, taking in what she said. I didn't see myself ever being married. Hell, I didn't even know what life had planned for us. I did know that life with Kash didn't seem too bad, and this year with him was going to be one for the books. So far, we had been through enough trouble to last us for several years. I prayed that this brought us closer because, honestly, a year with him didn't seem like enough time for me.

Kash's mom and dad didn't know anything about the year

thing we had going on, and I was happy about that. Kasha meant more to me than just this one-year stand. We always said we would forever be, and I wanted us to be more than friends forever. I wanted to be his everything. That scary moment made me realize that I was accepting less and needed to start taking what was mine.

Kasha was rightfully mine, and I was going to own that. No one could have him, and I didn't want anyone to have me. Standing up from my seat at the island in his kitchen, I walked back to the couch and sat next to him. The look on his face allowed me to see that he was in deep thought.

"You know I wouldn't want to go through this with nobody but you? I'm fucked up inside, and you never once tried to leave me because of what you had to endure on the strength of me. Even if you thought it, you never said it to anyone. I don't want to look for a house by myself. I want you to help me. I can't be in this place for longer than a week, so please don't take long. We not taking any of this shit either. I don't trust it. We can buy everything new. Whatever you want," he said and wrapped his good arm around me.

Kasha had been shot seven times, once in the leg, twice in his hand, twice in the arm, once in the chest, and the last one in the ankle. They wanted to take my man, but they didn't. God had to know I needed him, and not just for what he taught me, but because I felt like I would never find a love like this again. Kash was the man in my eyes, and nobody was better. His bullet wounds only made him that much finer to me. My man was a survivor, and I was going to make sure he got back to himself.

"Capri really did that shit?" he asked me, and I nodded. "I just needed you to confirm what I thought I remembered. I guess everybody ain't meant to go to the top with you."

CHAPTER TEN

KASH

It felt good to be out of the hospital and back in my bed. It felt even better being next to my bitch and knowing she had tried to do things while a nigga was in the hospital. I respected that she had my dad teach her things about the company, so she could handle it while I was in the hospital, and even while I was doing therapy.

I had been the one carrying it for her, and it felt good to know she didn't just leave me when I was down bad. Instead, she stepped up and handled business like a real woman should. Of course, I was mad at her but madder at myself that I didn't watch my surroundings better and I didn't see that shit coming. Amarie had found the house she wanted, and I had my dad make the call for us to get the paper work done. I knew Amarie was capable of doing it, but my father had gotten things done faster. His name in the realty world got him through doors fast. So, when he put a bid on something, he always got it.

Today, I had all the furniture and things Amarie picked out delivered to that house. Since my mom and Emily hadn't left, I had them decorating for me. I gave Emily two thousand dollars just to help my mom out. I couldn't wait to see the look on Amerie's face, but first I had some things to handle with Von. My crutches were limiting my moves, but that didn't mean anything.

Von picked the perfect time to get things done. The girls were going out for drinks tonight, and while they were out, we were going to pay this Terrell guy a visit. He kept saying I killed his sister when I had no clue who he was talking about. I wasn't a killer, and I could remember the very few people I did have to do something to. None of them were females. I didn't believe in hitting females, let alone killing them.

"Baby, are you ready for therapy? The guy is on his way," Amarie said as she came into the living room and started folding blankets.

We hadn't slept upstairs since I had been back home, simply because everything was easier to get to downstairs. I had already put this house on the market and was getting big offers. I got the house for a little over three hundred thousand, but with all the upgrades and things I put into it, I was asking for five hundred. People were already asking to come and see the place. I was going to leave the furniture and allow whoever moved in to decide if they wanted to keep it or not. I already had my safes taken out and moved to the other spot. A lot of my money was in the banks; however, I had cash for emergencies that would last me years before I ran out. I was big on saving in all forms.

"Yeah, I'm ready. When I'm done, we have to swing by this house and see if it's still the one you want. My dad went by already. He said it was nicer than it looked on the computer. It's a little further out, but the gated community is something I really want just to up the security measures."

"Okay. I'm going upstairs to shower and get myself

together while you do that. By the time I'm done with my stuff, you should be already started with your sessions. We ran out of fruit, so I'm going to grab some. Within that time, you should be ready. I put some outfits and stuff in the bathroom down here for you. If it's not what you want to wear, I can always change things."

"I need my dick sucked," I admitted.

Amarie looked at me and smiled. She kissed my neck, sliding her tongue across it. That motion alone had my dick on brick. My legs may have been a little off, but my dick was still going strong. Her hands traveled under my hoodie and over the bottom of my stomach. She smiled when I inhaled deeply at her touch. Amarie often told me how she loved the fact that it didn't matter when or how she touched me, I still reacted the same.

I watched carefully as Amarie lowered herself onto her knees while unbuckling my pants. She slowly pulled my dick out and let spit fall from her lips to the mushroom shaped head of my dick, which was leaking pre cum. Guiding my tool into her mouth, she moaned aloud. I held my moan in and enjoyed the feel of her warm, wet mouth. She let her head bob at a steady pace while swirling her tongue around him at the same time. She then pulled off, making a popping sound.

When Amerie looked up at me, we locked eyes, and she turned on demon mode. She slowly started to suck me back into her mouth. The way she bobbed and jerked had my toes about to bust out of my socks.

"Shit," I hissed.

She had pulled me out of her mouth and then started working her hands in opposite directions. My head fell back, and I grabbed the side of the couch to keep myself upright. I was holding on so tightly that I was sure my knuckles had turned white. She let some more spit fall from her lips onto me then started to suck on the head, only making the popping noise when she pulled off me. She loved sucking my dick just as much as I loved her doing it. Every time, she made sure it was as wet and sloppy as possible.

Amerie grabbed my waist, making me pump inside her mouth, being sure to let me hit the back of her throat. I wasted no time gaining a rhythm of my own as I made love to her throat. She was gagging, but she loved when that happened. Amerie often told me that sucking my dick was one of her favorite things to do.

Stopping me, she took back full control. This girl eased her head up and down and back and forth, all at a slow, steady pace. It looked to me like she was practicing breathing techniques before swallowing me whole and holding me there to hum for a second. When she pulled back her eyes were watering, but she refused to wipe them.

"Argh, fuck!" I hissed.

At that point, my knees gave out on me. They buckled, and my cum shot down her throat. My bitch swallowed every inch before standing up. She even tucked my now soft dick back inside my pants just as the doorbell rang. I looked at my phone and we both saw my trainer standing outside. Instead of opening the door, she unlocked it and told him to come in.

"Hey, have a good day," Amarie spoke before jogging up the stairs to probably get herself together.

"What's up?" my trainer spoke as he placed the mat on the floor.

"I'm good. Was just about to go to the bathroom," I replied.

I needed to wipe my dick off. Amarie had used so much spit that I could feel the shit on my boxers and running down my legs.

"Okay. I'll just set up while you go do that. We are going to do a lot of stretches, so you'll probably need to take some pain meds. Just like last time, if it becomes too much, and the pain is unbearable, we can stop."

I went into the bathroom and pissed before taking a rag and washing off my dick. After I cleaned my hands, I walked back out of the bathroom. Today would be hard because my knees already felt weak. I really wanted to crawl on the couch and go to sleep.

Sitting on the mats, we did a bunch of different stretches, which was easy at first. What bothered me was when he told me to stand up and reach down as far as I could. That took everything in me, and I didn't like it. We did that about three more times before he had me jogging very slowly around the living room. After a few walk arounds and tests, he wrapped his shit up and left me to go wash my ass. I got in the shower and cleaned myself up before I slowly pulled my clothes on.

Amarie had laid me out a pair of black Nike sweats with the matching hoodie. Once I had my clothes on, relaxed in the living room and waited for Von.

"Wake yo' ass up." I felt Von shaking my leg.

Lifting my head, I looked at him with a dumb expression. Von was standing at the top of the couch, using the crutch to nudge me.

"Nigga, I'm woke. Cut that shit out. We out or what?" I asked.

"Yeah, come on. Amarie just left not too long ago. I sat here and let you sleep while I took a few phone calls. Your ass was in here snoring like a hibernating bear." He laughed.

"Man, fuck you." I pushed myself up, and he handed me my crutch. I was going to use only one today.

We made it outside to his car, and I climbed in. The first thing I did was grab his blunt out the ashtray. I sparked it up and took a few deep pulls, causing me to cough. I hadn't smoked since I had been home from the hospital.

"Pass that shit. So, look. I got the nigga who did this to you, and that's where we on our way to. I been barely feeding his ass and fucking with him. I was going to just kill him, but I wanted you to make that call," he said as he pulled off.

Von had the kind of driving that made you want to put on a seatbelt. He barely stopped at stop signs, and he often went around cars and whatever else. I didn't even know why I agreed to get in the car with him. I held onto the handles above my head that we called the 'oh shit' handles as he sped around a trolley.

"Bro, that's illegal as hell," I reminded him.

"Relax," he simply said and plucked the ashes off his weed.

The weed wasn't even helping me relax, and the more my high kicked in, the more I felt like he was going to kill us. Finally, the car came to a complete stop, and I smiled. We were on the block, and I knew I was about to go down to the basement and have some fun.

After getting out of the car, we walked inside the house. I slapped hands with a few people before I limped down the stairs. Usually, the basement didn't have any smell, but today it smelled like shit and chicken, which was not a good mixture. The Popeyes box on the floor indicated his ass was eating good. I just hoped they were feeding him them dry ass biscuits with no juice nor water to wash them down.

"Damn, Terrell. What's up, my guy? I didn't think we would ever get a chance to meet. I hear you got a lot to say about me, and I want to hear about it," I said, pulling up a chair to sit directly in front of him.

Terrell looked up at me, and I instantly knew who he was. A big flash from my past came rushing to the forefront of my brain. I never knew his name, and I never killed his sister.

CHAPTER ELEVEN
KASH

"Kash, do the underdog thing one more time. This time, go higher," Carmen yelled as she laughed.

I ran around the swing and held on to it, running back then running forward before using all my strength to push it up high. While Carmen was in the air, I dipped underneath the swing to watch her go high.

"Woahhhh," she screamed.

Carmen was my friend from school. We were in the same class. Most people said we had a crush on each other, and while I thought she was the prettiest girl in the world, I liked her as my friend.

"One more time, Kasha. Please, this the last time." She giggled, and I ran over to give her one more push.

I heard the teachers calling us to line up, so we could go back across the street to school.

"Come on, Carmen, we have to go. I'll push you three times tomorrow," I said, wanting to get in the line and not get in trouble.

"This the last one. I want to back flip off this time," she said.

Against my better judgment, I pushed her. Carmen went to do a back flip, and I watched in amazement. I hadn't even gotten to the *point that I could flip off the swing. I was too scared I wouldn't land right. Just as fast as Carmen went up, she was coming down.*

Bonnngggg. The sound was loud, but the scream from my mouth was louder. Carmen had hit her head on the bar of the swing set. I tried to catch her, but her head smacked the ground before I could make it close enough.

"Oh, God! What happened?" My teacher, Mrs. Darby, ran over to us.

"It's my fault. She asked me to push her. She wanted to flip!" I cried.

There was so much blood pouring from her head that it made me sick to my stomach. My teacher tried to stand in front of me, so I couldn't see her, but that did nothing to the images in my head of her flying off that swing and smacking the pole before hitting the ground.

"I didn't kill your sister. That was an accident."

"Yes, you did. I remember they said you pushed her, even when it was time to go. You kept pushing her, and high," he insisted.

"She wanted me to push her. That was years ago. I was nine at the time. You don't know the trauma I endured from that. I didn't even know her family. We were friends in school. That girl was my best friend. I had to go through therapy to forgive myself and understand that me pushing her didn't make her jump off that swing," I told him.

Terrell looked at me before he spat in my direction. It landed a few feet from me, and before I knew it, I had grabbed him by his neck and yanked him toward. I slammed the hammer that I grabbed off the table into the side of his head. When I pushed him back, the chair he was in fell over.

Even tied down to a chair, and knowing he was about to die, he still talked shit. This man was still yelling about how he was going to kill me or even come back from the dead and haunt me until I drove myself crazy. I set the chair upright before grabbing the pair of pliers. Holding them next to his head, I locked them bitches on his ear. I don't know why I did it, but I knew when my mom used to grab me by the ear, that shit hurt.

Hearing him scream out in pain did something to me. It was like I wanted him to beg for his life. However, that wasn't me, and I never wanted to be that person.

"Von, do what you please to him. You know this is not how I operate."

I felt like that shooting was my karma for all the things I had done, and I wanted a clean slate with shit. I didn't care to kill him, as long as he didn't try and kill me again. However, something told me that he wouldn't leave me alone, and leaving him alive was only playing with my own life.

"Yeah, bitch. You know you can't do it. You couldn't kill me. You always been a punk. Portraying like you with that real life street shit. You only got street cred because of Von. Don't nobody in the hood respect you, and it's gon' always be like that!" he screamed.

Grabbing the gun off the table, I aimed it at his head and put a hole perfectly in the center. Seeing his head slump down, I frowned. I didn't want to kill him, but that was one thing I hated. People seemed to only respect you when you had a gun in your hand and they didn't. I put my work in, but I did it silently. I wasn't a killer and never claimed to be. I didn't want any parts of the street life, but I would never sell my friend out, and if he needed me, I wouldn't hesitate to jump into the field like I did a few times back in the day for him.

"You know you ain't have to do that, right? You could have let him pop his shit. He wanted you to kill him. Don't look at it like you did something bad. It was you or him, and you chose yourself. Anybody would have done that," Von said.

"I know you right. It doesn't make that shit easier, though," I said as I gagged before all the food that I had consumed this morning came up.

"One day you ain't gon' throw up no more, and the shit will be normal." Von laughed.

"Nah, that shit will never be normal to me. You crazy and love this life. I'll never judge you because this is who you are, but this ain't me."

We walked out of the spot and back to Von's car. I told him to take me past my office, so I could get things back in order. I knew Amarie had done some work for me, but I was sure a bunch of shit needed to be done that she couldn't do. We pulled up to my office half an hour later, and I dapped Von up. Using my crutches, I hopped my ass into the office and on the elevator. I stopped by each cubicle of my workers and directly spoke to them. When I walked into my office, I was surprised to see that it had been cleaned up, and my files were stacked neatly on my desk.

"Hey, Boss, glad to see you back. People have been reaching out nonstop about that new house you just put on the market. I have an offer for about six hundred thousand. Also, the contractors for the apartment complex finished the job. I didn't want to reach out to you, so when your dad came in, he assisted Amarie and showed her how to pay them through the company's account. So, that's done for you. Two houses sold a few days ago, thanks to Amarie as well. She's been in here helping us out. I don't know who trained her, but she's really good. She sort of moves like you but is way nicer. Each morning, she made sure the staff room was full of breakfast foods and coffee. If we stayed late, she made sure to send us food. I think we want to keep her in the office." Britt smiled.

"Oh, I'm going to give her something to show her our appreciation as a company. What do you suggest?" I asked.

"Maybe a raise or something, I would say, but she doesn't even work here. How about you offer her a position or something? We need her here because she does so well."

"She's starting her own company, so she's not going to come over here. I did buy her a house, so that may be something she's excited about. Maybe I could write her a check or gift her a property from the company."

"If she's starting her company, why don't you just write her a check, so she can furnish her place or maybe even hire a few people. I'm sure she could do something with the money," she said just as Amarie walked into my office.

Britt pulled her into a hug before exiting my office.

"What are you doing here? We were supposed to meet back at home to go over to this place," Amarie said as she came over and kissed my lips.

"I'm tending to my business, which I hear you have taken over and have my employees not wanting you to leave. Since you've been here doing all my work, what's up with your company?" I asked.

"I've been somewhat working on it. It's just better here. I was thinking that maybe we could merge the companies, or you could buy into my company. Then I would be able to pay my mom a lump sum to get her off my back. I have her meeting me here if that's okay. I know I should have asked you first, but I feel more comfortable here since it's all these people," she said, and I nodded.

"Whatever you want, you know I got you."

I admired her beauty. Amarie could have asked me for a million dollars, and the way she made me feel, I would have only asked her if she wanted it on her card or in cash. I knew I was falling in love with her, but that one-year thing still stood in the shadows.

"Hey, Amarie, your mother is here with your father. Should I send them up?" Britt's voice came over the speaker.

"Yes, please do. I also need you to call and double check that those pizzas and wings will still be delivered by five. I know some people are leaving a little early today since everyone stayed behind last night," she responded like this was her shit.

"Okay, love."

A few seconds later, the arguing couple walked into the room.

Amarie was now seated in the chair next to me while I typed away on my laptop. I was reaching out to clients as well as sending out emails to some of my tenants who were past due on their rent.

"Well, hello. I see you finally reached out," her mother said.

"Let's close the door, and you two can take a seat, so we can discuss why you're really here." Amarie motioned with her hands for them to sit down.

Her dad proudly smiled at her while her mother plopped in the chair like a misbehaving toddler. Amarie remained silent as they sat down.

"Just to get to it, I did reach out, and the reason why is that I want to buy you out. I know your husband stands with you, and maybe he can help you see that taking this money and leaving me alone is what's best. I've been so focused on pleasing you and everyone else in my life that I didn't make myself happy. I haven't even reached my full potential yet, and I barely got the company off the ground, and you are already taking me to court. As your child, I feel like that's selfish of you, but I've been learning that it's the people closest who do you the dirtiest. I want to handle this outside of court, since I'm about to go through a big divorce, and I know he's going to come for my money, just as you have. The only difference is, I can come back for his, while you have nothing for me to countersue for, and you being in my life isn't something I can get back," Amarie started.

She was leaned back in the chair, looking her mother directly in her eyes.

"How much?" Amarie's mother asked.

"I'll give you a total of one hundred thousand over two years. Fifty thousand a year," Amarie offered, and I knew her ass just threw a number out there.

"Deal," her mom said.

Amarie slid a contract across the table and had her mother sign it.

That woman's eyes lit up like a kid on Christmas, while Amerie's father didn't look pleased. He didn't even look like he wanted to be there.

"Amarie, whatever you decide to give her, that's what she will get. That business is yours, and the least we can do is watch you prosper. Yes, she is my wife, but you are my child. I want you to understand that I don't agree with what she's doing, and if she takes this money from you, I will divorce her the day she cashes that check." Her father stood and made his way out the door.

"Guess I better get ready to be left." Her mom smiled and walked out behind him.

"Don't worry about how you're going to get the money. I'll buy into your company. Two million sound like enough?" I asked.

This dumb ass girl's face went pale before she hit the floor with a loud thud.

I grabbed my water and tossed it on her face before lightly tapping her a few times. Amarie's eyes opened, and she looked at me. Using all my strength, I pulled her up to her feet.

"Don't do that shit no more. I told you I got you forever."

CHAPTER TWELVE

NAKARI

S itting in the back of the car, I looked out the window as we drove through the hood. Today was the day Capri's family decided to lay her to rest. Amarie sat beside me, rubbing my hand. She had a stale look on her face. I knew she didn't want to be there, but she was, on the strength of me. Kash was beside her, holding onto her hand, and I had to admire his strength. He had ditched his crutches but still had a slight limp in his walk.

Amarie often told me how hard things were for him with his recovery, yet to everyone else, he made it seem like things were going great. I was all cried out and could no longer shed any tears. Capri's family didn't go all out like I expected, and the funeral wasn't long. A lot of people came out to show their respects, and even more were outside on the streets.

I looked at all the cars behind us and in front of us as we drove down Baltimore Ave to the cemetery, Capri's final resting place. Cars were honking, and people were hanging out of their sunroofs. Everyone was showing Capri mad love. Kash nor Von had spoken on what she'd done, and no one in the streets knew what happened to her except that she was shot. I had even more respect for them for keeping things quiet. Had it been me, I wouldn't have been quiet about anything, and I would have made it known what was really going on.

The moment we pulled into the something seemed to break inside of Von. He didn't cry, but he let it be known that he wasn't getting the fuck out of the car. We all looked at him but said nothing. One by one, we stepped out. The way Capri's family had it, by the time people were getting out of their cars, they were already carrying her royal blue casket over to put her in the ground.

"Ashes to ashes, dust to dust," was the only thing I remembered hearing.

I watched as females cried just like I was crying the other day. Some even wore pictures of the two on their shirts, letting me know they weren't just friends. Everywhere I looked, I saw someone crying. I felt like I couldn't breathe. Quickly going back over to the car, I slid down the side and started crying again. Looking at all those females, I wondered if maybe what we had wasn't even real. Capri had so many chicks, and they all were comforting each other.

"That girl was a true nigga." Kash came over to me and spoke. "Her having all those females don't take away how she felt for you. Don't let that shit get to you. Of course, all of them bitches were going to show up like that, even if the only thing Capri did was send them a text. You got to be strong and stand on all ten. Everybody knew what was up with y'all. Don't let nobody see you fold," he told me and reached out to help me up.

I grabbed his hand and stood to my feet.

We walked back over just as they began to drop roses on her casket. There were so many falling off. I decided not to drop a rose since I didn't want to be that close. I noticed an older lady who had a look of disgust on her face, and I immediately recognized her as Capri's mother. She looked just like her, and Capri always spoke about how her mother would never accept that her daughter didn't want to be in a dress, which was exactly why she was laid up in that casket with one on.

Capri looked like a bad bitch. However, that wasn't her. I knew Capri's ass would have wanted some expensive jeans, a fitted cap, and a crazy shirt that matched some shoes that nobody had.

We all stood back for a while until everybody started piling into their cars.

"Excuse me, are you Narkari?" a girl walked up to me and asked.

"Why, what's up?" I questioned her.

"I just wanted to let you know that I'm Capri's wife. Her mother and family know this. Hell, everyone knew but you. I reached out to you a few times on Instagram. Maybe you never saw the messages?" She placed her hand on her hip.

"Wife? Girl, stop. Were y'all going through a divorce or something? I've been to Capri's house, and there were no signs of you. We are at a funeral, hers to be exact, and you pick this time to approach me? You have no class," I added.

"Yes, wife. I have that girl's last name and all. We have a two-year-old child. Capri had a family, and you tried to step in and take that from me." She started to get loud, causing people to look over at us.

"I didn't know about you, don't know you, and at this point, neither of us have her. You approaching me about someone who is present with the Lord." I mocked the one thing I heard at every funeral.

"Bitch, I will kill you." She flashed her gun.

That made me laugh. She was doing all that for no reason at all. It wasn't like I was gon' keep seeing her. Neither of us would. Of course, I felt some type of way; I was upset inside. Hell, Capri had a lot going on. She could have at least told me about this shit and let me decide if I wanted her to keep eating me like I was her last meal.

"Now you just want to send me up there to your wife. You want us to be together forever, huh? Look, I'm going to go. I'm sorry for your loss. You should go seek some comfort from your in laws." I turned to walk away.

I felt her snatch my head back, and a few punches landed. There was no way I would let this lady just beat my ass. Turning my body as much as I could, I started to throw my own punches, landing them wherever I could.

"These bitches are classless," I heard.

"Now if my bitches don't fight for me, even when I'm gone, I ain't doing it right," someone else said while others yelled that they were going live.

Using all my strength, I pushed forward, making her go backward. I knew we were going to hell for fighting in a damn cemetery.

"You should have left me alone. I don't fucking know you! Now I got to beat your ass while you have your gun on you," I said, punching her as hard as I could in the back of her head.

"Dust that bitch!" I heard Natalia yell.

I delivered some mean uppercuts to her face that had the crowd yelling, "Damn!" After a few of those punches to the face, she was screaming a different tune.

"Get this bitch off me. Help me, please!" she screamed.

"Nah, I told you I didn't want no problems, hoe. I ain't know shit about you. Now you gon' take all this." I slung her body to the ground.

"That's it. Put them fucking phones down. Ain't shit cool about this," Von's voice boomed loudly.

Letting the girl go, I stepped back to look at my damage.

Her face wasn't as bad as it could have been, but she was bleeding. Walking over to the car, I climbed in, ready to go home. This was by far the worst funeral, and it had to be that Capri was still getting her karma since she couldn't even be peacefully laid to rest. I would have rather watched some other bitches fight over her, not be one of them.

"What happened?" Amarie asked.

"She approached me. I ain't know that girl was married, and she wasn't moving like it. I told the girl I ain't want no problems and even tried to walk away. She grabbed my hair, and I gave her exactly what she was asking for. I was only up there because I wanted to be closer, yet at the same time far enough to watch everything. This girl was going hard too, talking 'bout she will kill me." We shared a laugh because she didn't even have to do all that.

"Excuse me, I have to ask that you all leave," a guy in a purple suit said.

"Please go and tell your mother we will leave in a second. Also, let her know she did homie fucked up by putting her in that damn Cinderella gown. We all know y'all should have swapped outfits at least." Von sent him on his way.

The whole funeral was a disaster, and I somehow wished I had never even come. About fifteen minutes later, everyone was back in the car, and we had all decided to go back to the block. Well, they decided for me. Kash had decided to throw a cookout in memory of Capri, while Von, on the other hand, said fuck her.

"Aye, Kash, you knew she had a wife but failed to mention it when you were giving your pep talk."

"I didn't know what you knew and didn't know. And, yes, they were married. I don't usually get into people's business, but you can't get the answers from who owes you them. Capri married her to spite her parents. She always did stuff to make them mad. She said they weren't together, but that could be a lie. I wasn't too aware of what she did with her strap. Capri surprised us all. A few months ago, I would have told you don't worry because one thing about her, she was loyal, but hell, even that's not true. Don't sit here and cry over a bitch that ain't here. She was a goofy, and even though I forgive her and ain't want to see her dead, I don't have anything nice to say about her. I don't even really want to be doing this, but the real one in me ain't gon' let who I thought was my friend go out like that," Kash explained as Amarie walked over and pecked his lips.

"You okay, cousin?" she asked me.

"Yeah. I need a triple shot of Henny and an ounce of weed to smoke to the face," I admitted.

I wasn't used to dealing with drama. I didn't even do relationships, nor did I get this close to people. In my mind, females were worse than males. This girl hid shit from me so perfectly that I almost didn't believe she was married. I mean, not the way she was acting over me. How she flaunted me through the hood and had me all up in her house. I didn't care if it was to make her family mad or not, I felt like that was information she should have shared with me.

"Get out yo' head. You know the vibes, sis. It's always fuck these hoe ass niggas." Natalia came over with a bottle and three shot cups.

"Exactly. All we know is free the guys." Amarie smiled, quoting a Philly rapper as we all grabbed a shot and tossed it back.

Natalia quickly filled them back up, and we tossed another one.

"Don't get your head knocked off." Von looked at Natalia with an expression that said he wasn't playing.

Natalia poured another round and raised her glass to him.

"Stand on what you believe in, sis, and never let a nigga play you. If he on shit, then you be on shit too. Hell, I may need to come on the other side of the rainbow and see what's it's like over there." Natalia laughed while looking at Von.

"You want a bitch? We can go get one. Point one out, and I bet you I can get her to please both of us. You know what we on, so I'm gon' let you pop your shit for now. They know who bed you gon' be in tonight." He laughed at her before walking off.

I watched my family as they looked at their men with love in their eyes. I wanted that, and like always, I was the one who didn't get it. I was slightly jealous in a way. However, I was happy for them and knew that when it was my time, the person for me would be for me.

CHAPTER THIRTEEN

AMARIE

I inhaled the smoke and leaned down to kiss his lips.

I licked Kash's bottom lip, and with that, he deepened the kiss. I slowly moved my hips on his hard dick, loving the feeling. Pulling away to catch my breath, I smiled down at him. He placed the rest of what he was smoking in the ashtray and grabbed my hips.

Kash pulled my hair down from its clip and started to kiss my neck, causing a low moan to leave my mouth. His left hand slid under my shirt and bra, squeezing my breasts and then rubbing my now hard nipples one at a time. His other hand found its way inside my sweatpants, and he slowly rubbed my pearl through my panties.

"Awwww, shit." I moaned, leaning my head back as I moved against his hands.

After pulling off my pants and panties, Kash slid his seat as far back as it could go. He lifted me, surprising me with the strength in his arms. He moved me just enough so I could sit on his face.

My ass continuously moaned as Kash licked and sucked on

my clit. "Ride my face," he said as he slid one finger into me, moving it in and out as he sucked on my throbbing clit. "OHHH GODDDDDD!" I screamed while rotating my hips on his face.

He inserted another finger and picked up the pace. My body began to shake, and my hips bucked as I came all over his face, but his tongue never came out, nor did he stop sucking and nibbling. I'd never had this feeling before. It felt like at any moment, I would pass out from this feeling that I never wanted to stop. My stomach tightened as he kept eating me, and the only sound was his slurping and smacking and my low whimpers, begging him not to stop.

I screamed when my body started to shake uncontrollably. "Let it out, Ma," Kash coached as he placed his mouth back on me, pressing his tongue against my pearl really hard and moving his fingers in a come here motion. I felt like I had to pee.

"STOP, BABY! I HAVE TO PEE. DAMN, I CAN'T TAKE IT! I CAN'T TAKE NO MORE. I'M SORRY. AHHHHHHHHH, SHIT! I'M SO SORRY!" I yelled as tears fell from my eyes. I didn't even know why I was sorry, but I was.

I felt my body jerk as I squirted all over his face. Kash laughed and helped me down off his face, licking his lips in the process.

"I made your ass apologize for no reason." He smiled, looking satisfied. My ass had to wipe away tears I didn't even know were falling. "Damn, Ma, I made you cry," he said, wiping his face with the napkins he had pulled from somewhere in the car.

"Shut up," I mumbled as I put my clothes back on.

"What?" Kash said as he acted like he would pick me back up. "Noooo... noooo, I can't take no more. We need to get inside and have a good time with your parents before they go back go home." I laughed as I moved back into my seat, exhausted like I had just run a marathon.

"I'm just fucking with you. Damn, you can't handle my mouth no more?" He cracked a big smile.

"Do you have any more shirts in your car?"

"Nah, why?" he asked as he sparked his blunt back up.

"Umm, your shirt is soaked with my juices, and I'm not trying to go into your parents' place with you like that." Kash turned his car off and pulled his shirt off. "It's cool." He smirked, looking at me.

I was now balled up in the seat with my eyes low but trained on him.

"You tired?" he asked when I yawned.

I wanted to nod my head yes, but instead, I said no. Had I said yes, we would have been on our way back home.

After fixing ourselves as best we could, we walked into the house and greeted everyone. I was happy to see that his family was all there. However, when I heard my auntie and cousins, I knew it was about to be a great time. My auntie knew how to party, and her daughters took after her. We made our rounds through the entire house before we made our way into the kitchen. I was hoping his dad had made some yams and baked macaroni because his shit was so good.

When I saw the marked pans, I smiled. I knew exactly what I was getting, and I was going to have a nice plate. While Kash took a seat, I grabbed two plates and filled them both with foods we liked. I walked the plates over to the table, then I went back and grabbed him a beer and myself a little wine cooler.

"Damn, babe, who gon' eat all this?" Kash asked.

I looked at him like he was crazy.

We sat quietly eating our food until I couldn't take anymore. I'd had enough and was ready to drink and mingle with everyone else. Kash had again left his crutches, and I knew sooner or later he was going to be limping around and complaining about his leg hurting. The moment he did, we would leave, so he could take his meds and go to bed. Kash could never just take his pain pills and go on about his day, which was why he didn't like taking them. The moment he dumped those pills, his ass fell fast asleep wherever he was.

"I'm gon' clean this mess up. You want to go hang with the ladies? You know my mom and your auntie probably smoking up all Von's weed. I swear they asses need to slow down." He laughed.

The very few times we'd gotten our families together, my aunt and Mrs. Kristie had dipped off and would be smoking up so much weed when we found them. Their asses would be stuck laughing at a bunch of nothing. I knew they were high when they started telling each other hilarious stories that they had already laughed about.

Leaving Kash in the kitchen to clean up our mess, I went over to my cousins and his, who were all surrounding the bar.

"Let's go. It's time to get fucked up!" Nakari yelled.

I was happy just to see her smile. I knew we all were going through some shit, and each thing was hitting us hard. It was like we were playing dodge ball with life being the one throwing the ball at all our heads. Nobody was winning right now, and it was time we got rid of all the negative energy. So, when my baby had finally made it over to us, and we all had our shots in the air, I spoke up.

"To life not getting us down anymore. To picking our heads up and utilizing our time left on this bitch better."

"I'll drink to that," Natalia said as we clinked glasses before throwing the shots back.

It seemed like every time we took a shot, Natalia filled the glasses right back up.

The strong effects of the alcohol were long gone, and we were now just knocking drinks down. The music was blasting, and weed was in rotation. Everyone was full of laughs, and this was a time we needed.

"What the hell you doing, babe? Why you got all these cups filled? What's in them?" Von asked Natalia.

"Let's see how fast we can drink them. Whatever cup you pick up, you have to drink. It's a number inside, and that's how many shots you get," Natalia said as she downed her first cup and walked back to the bar to probably pour more rounds.

Nakari quickly followed her. I found myself drinking cup after cup nonstop along with everyone else at the bar. Natalia's ass thought she was a bartender and was feeding everybody Hennessy. I could tell that Kash was drunk too.

"Amarie, come here, baby. I miss you," Kash said as he lifted me and placed me on the bar. It had to be the alcohol because he usually had a little pain when he lifted me. Now, he was doing it with ease.

"What do you want?" I giggled.

Completely past drunk, I kissed him like we were the only two in the room, and of course, he matched my energy. Kash pulled me down off the bar, and we walked further back into the basement where there was a door that led to a movie room. He was still shirtless, and I licked down his body, tracing the line of his boxers and causing him to suck in a breath. Kash lifted me on top of the mini bar in the corner of the room. He then pulled my shirt over my head.

After quickly placing a soft kiss to my lips, he traveled his tongue down from my neck, stopping between my breasts, making my body shiver. He licked around my nipples, causing them to get cold, and then placed a kiss on each boob. I was now breathing hard and ready for him to fuck me silly.

"Ohhh," a moan slipped from my lips.

Kash moved his tongue all over my exposed skin. I pushed him back and reached over to grab the cup I had brought with me.

"Nah, ma, you already drunk enough," he said as he held onto my waist.

I looked down into Kash's face as my fingers rubbed his chest.

"You're soo fucking beautiful, babe. I love you so much, and I'm so thankful for you. I want to give you everything you need in a woman," I slurred, biting my lip. I had to tell him how I really felt. I giggled at the sound of my voice.

"Move up," Kash told me, almost in a groan.

He slid off the barstool and pulled me, so I was for the second time hovering over his face. I didn't know when he got my bottoms off, but I was happy he did.

He started to lick the inside of my thighs. My moans only seemed to turn him on. I leaned my body back and held onto the end of the bar. With the room spinning around me, I was sure I would fall over if I didn't hold on. Kash slid me closer to him and began to lick my clit. I threw my head back and moaned.

Sticking his tongue inside me, he moved his head back and forth, so he was tongue fucking me. "Shit, Kasha!" I screamed as I got that familiar feeling in my stomach again.

"Well, god damn, this what the hell all that screaming was about," Nakari said, making me jump. I damn near fell off the bar.

Kash only smacked his teeth, then lifted his head from between my legs and rested it on my stomach. We waited for her to say something, but she never did.

"Nakari, what the fuck could yo' ass possibly fucking want?" Kash half-yelled, mad that she'd interrupted our long-awaited playtime.

I was sure if I hadn't gotten scared, he wouldn't have stopped. He seemed not to care who was watching; he only wanted to please me. Hell, I didn't care at the moment if she watched. I just didn't want him to stop.

"From the looks of it, both of you are drunk as hell, and I was coming to tell you that your dad is here and asking to speak with you," she said.

I knew when she started to laugh that it was because of my drunk ass. I was trying to put my clothes on but failing miserably. They both burst out laughing when I tried to put my pants on and fell over. My whole ass was in the air, and I was stuck. Both of those dummies were too busy laughing to help me, though.

CHAPTER FOURTEEN

AMARIE

S tanding in front of my dad, I wasn't sure what to say. He looked like he was stressed, and I kind of understood why. If I had a wife like his, I would be upset too.

"Princess, I miss you. I'm sorry for what you are going through. I knew you would think I was in on that money stuff with your mother, but I'm not. I promise to God, if and when she accepts that money from you, I'm leaving her. I already have my doubts about our relationship just off how she treats you alone, but when you have twenty plus years into someone, leaving them isn't as easy as it may seem. I could talk your head off about all the things I should have done or wish I did. I know that won't fix nothing, though. Just please continue to let me be in your life," he pleaded.

I didn't know if it was the alcohol or how I really felt, but tears quickly began to pour from my eyes.

"You know I always wanted a dad, always. Even when you weren't around, I knew that one day you would treat me like your child. I figured the money would stop being sent through Auntie, and you would reach out directly, but that never happened. You had my phone number, yet you never called me, always Auntie. I've let you both have so much say so in my life, and for what reason? That's your wife, so I wouldn't ask you to leave her. I simply just want her to leave me alone and you too if you want to play these back-and-forth games. I'm not a child anymore, and I don't need anyone to take care of me. I'm capable of doing what I need to do as an adult," I expressed to him.

For the first time in my life, I saw the hard look my dad always wore wash off his face and tears fall. My dad didn't even cry when his mom died. When my aunt told him, he came home, attended the funeral, and went back. My auntie always said that their mother wasn't shit, and that was the prime reason my dad went the route he did.

"I'm sorry, I really am. I don't know what to do or how to fix things. Since I've been back, I feel like our relationship has gotten worse and not better. I'm willing to make things right. Just tell me what you want me to do. What do you need from me?" he whispered.

"I just need you to try. Come around more, let's go places and get to know each other. You're my dad and nothing like the lady you've laid down and pro created with." I pulled him to me and hugged him.

"I'm really sorry, Princess. I never intended for things to be like this. I was trying to give you the best life I could while I was away. I'm not too fond of Philly. It seems like shit is just all the same. Traveling the world was what I wanted to do, and I did it. You're right. You've been living up to who we wanted you to become, and I truly hope you stop that and live for you. It's time you blossom into who you need to be. That man is good for you. Don't let him go, and don't change who you are for no one unless it's for you or to better yourself," my dad told me before he pulled away and wiped his tears.

"I won't, Dad. Why you are even out this late? Come on inside. You hungry? It's food and drinks. Loosen up and have a good time."

We walked inside the house, and I knew I needed a few more drinks. The ones I had in my system were starting to wear off. Grabbing the half full bottle of Hennessy, I poured us both a shot. I had never seen my dad drink, but when he tossed the shot back and didn't even react, I knew my alcohol problems had to have come from him. For the rest of the night, we all drank and partied until people started leaving or falling asleep. I knew my auntie was comfortable when I saw her hair tied up.

"Girl, this house is big as hell, and I don't feel like driving back home. I'm gon' go up there, take me a nap, and then take my ass home." She pulled me in for a hug.

My dad ventured off to the table where the older guys were playing dominos and started to have his own fun. I looked around at all the festivities. This night had come in perfect timing because it was exactly what we all needed.

CHAPTER FIFTEEN

NATALIA

I lay on the bed, staring up at Von. His eyes traveled over my face before landing on my body. I chewed on my bottom lip while watching him watch me. I had to squeeze my legs together because my middle was throbbing. I mean, I had a pulse between my legs that had me ready to do things to him that I hadn't even known I could do.

"I'm serious right now. How are you telling niggas you gon' pull up like you don't got me right here? What kind of hoe shit is you on?" he gritted.

"The same hoe shit you on," I replied.

"Man, you want me to fuck some shit up. That's what you want, Natalia?"

I didn't know if it was the hot ass in me, but the way my name rolled off his tongue turned me on. I couldn't keep giving in to him, though. He wanted me to be a wife while he still let bitches have their way with him, and I wasn't going for that.

I bit my bottom lip and shook my head no. For some reason, everything he said or did got my panties moist, and I hated it. If Von ever decided to turn his card in, I would be right with him, turning in mine, so we could be together forever. If not, we would just have to do our hoe shit and find a way to not let it get to the other person.

"Why you can't just be to me what you want me to be to you?" I asked him a serious question.

We both played a lot and got mad a lot too often about the same things. I hated when he was with me, and bitches blew his phone up. All he would do was silence his phone, and I would do the same.

Von looked at me and laughed, something he often did when he was about to avoid a question. His expression quickly changed into that deep frown that was going to give him permanent creases in his forehead.

"What you mean? I stick dick in you every night, and I make sure you good. So, who cares if I'm fucking other bitches? You knew I was doing that from the beginning," he said like it was okay.

"Yeah, that was before you wanted to show up at my job and act a fucking fool in the parking lot. You could have cost me my job, and then you think I'm just gon' sit around and be all for you while you do you? I'm supposed to be okay just because you climb in my bed every night? I actually feel bad for myself. If you can go out and fuck whoever, so can I. I only get dick and money from these niggas," I shot back.

"And while you are accepting their handouts, don't forget to tell them I'm handing out hollow tips. We are not the same, and what I do don't mean you can do it. Yeah, it sounds good, but you a bitch at the end of the day," he expressed.

"Watch your mouth. You run around with bitches. I'm a lady." I laughed at myself.

"You know what I mean." His expression softened.

"I'm not accepting that, Von, so if you go out here and kill people behind me, that's on you. You either all in with me or you not but expect the same thing from me. Now, I like you, and I like you a lot. So, I'm willing to do this relationship thing with you. But if you not, then this shit that we're doing can't continue. We can keep going on dates and talking, but you won't be in my bed every night and having me cook for you and all this other shit. We both hoes, baby," I admitted, and I wasn't lying.

I could pretend like I wanted to give the pussy up, and guys would give me whatever I wanted. I was okay with living life like that. However, I loved the feeling Von gave me. Climbing out of bed, I walked over to my closet and searched for something to wear. While I was in the closet, I sent Amarie and Nakari a text to see if they were still coming out.

I grabbed my high waisted denim Fashion Nova jean shorts and my orange wrap around cropped shirt. My wig was perfectly intact, so I just slicked down my baby hairs. The wig looked like it was coming straight from my scalp, and I loved it. After wrapping my scarf around my head, I went and took a quick shower.

I stepped into the shower, letting the hot water fall over my body. Although I wanted to get my hair wet, I decided against it. Tonight, I planned to go to the club with or without my girls. I heard Von as he walked into the bathroom and moved around. Finally, he stepped in the shower with me, and I let my eyes travel down his body. This man was perfect in every sense, but he wasn't mine, and it was time for me to stop acting like he was. He wasn't ready, even with all the mixed signals he gave off, and I damn sure wasn't about to force him to be ready.

We washed each other's bodies before he pulled me close to him, and my back rested against his chest. We stood there doing and saying nothing as the water fell on us.

Von turned me around and picked me up. He placed my

back against the shower wall, and we began to kiss each other passionately. Usually, this would lead to sex between us, but I wasn't having it, so I tapped his shoulder for him to let me down. He placed me back on my feet and stepped out of the shower.

"One second you kissing me like you want me to love on you, and the next you tapping me to put you down," Von seethed

"Me? Want you to love on me after the conversation we just had? Haha, no thank you, but I sure was ready to eat that dick up," I stated, shocking him.

He quickly got back in the shower, but his footing was off. Before I knew it, his ass was slipping and grabbing the shower curtain to break his fall. The look on his face had me doubled over with laughter.

"No, I don't want no dick now. It's too late." I smirked, stepping out of the shower and walking past him as he steadied himself.

I went into the room, dried myself off, and then sat on the bed, where I greased my body from head to toe.

Looking over at my outfit that I had gotten out earlier, I decided to switch it up a bit. Instead of going for some shorts, I was going to wear jeans. The moment I had it figured out, I slipped my clothes on and walked over to my vanity. Since I wasn't really big on too much makeup, I only did eyeliner and applied my favorite Mac matte Ruby Woo lipstick. I unwrapped my scarf and then put on my big hoop earrings. My blue Prada sneakers were the perfect match, and I felt like this was the perfect time to pop them out. They complemented my outfit too well for me not to wear them. I grabbed my bag and phone, then made my way to the front door. Von was on my heels as I went outside.

"Fuck is you going? We was supposed to be chilling in the crib tonight," he said.

"No, baby. I'm going out to eat and for a few drinks." I reminded him of the plans I told him about this morning that he thought he would come over and cancel.

"So, you not gon' stay in with me? I could fuck your pretty ass and feed you," he offered.

"Then that means I wasted a perfectly good outfit."

"No, you didn't, and stop playing with me like you really going outside." He grabbed me by my hips and pulled me to him, licking the side of my face.

"First of all, don't do that nasty shit again. I got dressed for nothing." I folded my arms over my chest.

"I'll go get dressed too then. Fuck it, you want me to put on some shit I never wore? I'm hungry as shit. We can order some food from Uber Eats and then let me eat you for dessert." He kissed me all over my face.

This was the part that had me falling for him in ways I didn't want or need to. Von was so soft and gentle with me sometimes, and other times, he was a fucking cocky bitch, and I wanted nothing to do with him. He often reminded me of myself, and that made me like him even more. We understood each other in ways nobody else could.

Sliding my hand down the front of his boxers, I had to laugh at myself before I let it run over his length. I'd give him a good nine and a half inches. Von knew like I knew that I was going to fuck him before we parted ways. I didn't care how much we went back and forth; his dick was too good for me to just let it pass me by.

Von let a low groan leave his lips before pulling me into the house and closing the door. He carried me over to the couch, and I lay on my back, watching as he slid off his boxers and pants. I eased my shorts and panties off and let my hand roam down to my clit. As I rubbed it in slow circles while biting my bottom lip, I thought about how I was going to get the dick and still go out. Hell, the way he put it down, my house was as good as his.

Von stood there staring at me while I finger fucked myself. I let my hand go back and forth, allowing loud moans to leave my lips. When he couldn't take watching me anymore, he slid the condom on and climbed between my legs.

That man spread my legs apart, then picked them up, wrapping them around his waist. Von's hands went to my waist, and he lifted me in the air.

"Let your body tilt back," he ordered.

Just like always, I did as he said when it was time to please my body. Von took his time entering me. I placed my hands on the couch to keep steady. It looked like I was in a half bridge. Von stroked me with deep, long strokes. I was in pure heaven as he crashed into my body.

"Keep playing with that shit, baby. Don't stop unless I tell you to. We gon' make that muthafucka squirt together."

He took my hand and placed my fingers back on my clit. I began to rub myself while he pumped in and out of me. I screamed as my body shook in his hands, and he began to thrust harder. Instead of going harder like he usually would, he bent down and kissed me. The way he kissed me made me dizzy, and I knew then that it was possible we felt more for each other than we cared to express.

"I'm not letting up on you. I swear to God," he spoke against my lips as he swirled his hips in circles, making my soul cry.

The way he gave me dick was like he was trying to ignite a flame in me that only he could put out. That flame that had me thinking irrationally, begging him not to leave, and meeting his family. Hell, I was ready to start one of our own if he told me that's what he wanted right now. I felt his body jerk, then he pulled out of me, took the condom off, and began to stroke his manhood. Being the nasty bitch I was, I slid down far enough for him to let go all over my face.

"Come get in the shower with me. I'm tired."

He pulled me up, and just like the dummy my fucked silly ass was, I went with him. For the first time, I cancelled my plans over a man.

CHAPTER SIXTEEN

KASH

If Amarie knew what I was doing, she would be mad, but I had to do it. DeJuan and his family had been quiet for too long, and I didn't like it. Knowing his family cared a great deal about their business, I knew how I had to play them, which is why her dad and I were at their house unannounced. I was going to come alone, but he called my phone, asking to meet up. When I told him what I was on my way to do, he begged to come.

Walking up to their front door, I knocked loudly. The door swung open, and DeJuan's father looked at us like we were lost.

"What are you doing here?" he asked, glancing around.

"We came to talk like men. Can we come in?" I requested.

He hesitated at first before stepping back and allowing us into his home.

"Welcome, sir," a maid greeted us, offering a glass of water, which I quickly turned down. They could have put some of that candy the whole family seemed to be addicted to in there, and I wanted no parts.

"This bitch is nice," Mr. Aaron said.

"Thank you. Have a seat, gentlemen," DeJuan's father said and sniffled.

"I'm here to see what we can do as far as this divorce with Amarie and DeJuan goes. He's been quiet for a while, and that's unlike him. I want to ensure that no more problems come her way, or I'll be sure to accidentally leak all the drug activity going on with him that you support. I'll also release the footage of your dear child, who still works in your firm, doing drugs in costumes and having wild sex with both men and women. I'd also hate for it to get out that you and Ms. Maid here share a child who is currently fourteen years old that you had shipped off to Mexico after doing a DNA test. I'm sure you don't want any of this to go floating around your office."

"I'll talk to him. We can settle this outside of court. Nobody will get anything, and both will walk away free. That's the only way we will agree. I refuse to let her have an ounce of money after she left him for dead," he said.

"That's all fine. She doesn't need your money. Have your son sign the papers and send them to my office. I'll make sure she gets them," I said as he rubbed his nose for what seemed like the thirtieth time.

"Perfect. Now, I'll have Ms. Eliza see you out. I have a meeting to attend." He all but ran up the stairs.

I was sure the meeting he spoke of had a lot to do with his nose.

Mr. Aaron and I walked out of the house and to my car. I found it funny that we both had a limp and were going around, making shit happen. Had it been me being pulled up on by two niggas with a limp, I probably would have had all the jokes in the world.

"Do you think Amarie would go if I asked her to dinner? I

just want to get to know her more. She's my child, and I barely know anything about her." He reached over and grabbed my lighter to light his cigarette.

I didn't allow cigarette smoking in my car or my house, simply because that smell was hard to get rid of, and they stunk, if you asked me. However, he may have needed a cigarette, and who was I to tell him not to get one?

"Look here, old man. I'm the only one dating her and getting to know her." I pulled my car over.

Mr. Aaron looked at me like I had lost my mind. Although I wanted to laugh, I kept up my antics.

"I'm glad you asked me could she go out, 'cause that's my bitch," I went to say.

Mr. Aaron tossed his cigarette out the window and fumbled with the door before he finally got it open.

"Come on! Get up out this bitch. Throw your dukes up. Who the fuck you think you is, young blood?" he said as I got out of the car and put my hands up.

He started rocking, bobbing, and weaving. I could tell he was lining his punch up.

Unable to hold it anymore, I burst out laughing. "I'm just fucking with you, old school."

Mr. Aaron looked at me, and I could tell he didn't find shit funny, which only made it funnier to me.

"You done made me waste my fucking cigarette, and that was my last one. I should slide your ass." He finally laughed before walking over to the car and getting back in.

"My bad. I just had to get you. Anybody ever tell you to loosen up? I know you spent a lot of time having to be hard all the time, but you ain't got to be like that. Everybody is all family and shit, so it's cool to laugh and joke."

It was quiet for a few minutes before he spoke again.

"Thanks, man. Thank you for making my daughter happy

and giving her a good life. I mean, you seem to have it all together. I appreciate you showing her that there's more to life, and even with the amount of money you have, you still treat her with respect and like she's human. Your family welcomed her with open arms, and that all I wanted for her." He looked me in my eyes while talking to me.

"No problem. She's giving me a lot too. All I ever wanted was for someone to love me for me and not for what I have. I will admit, things between us seem to be moving fast, yet it feels right. That girl means so much to me that I'm willing to do anything for her. Like pay her mom that hundred gees, just so she can leave her alone. I also don't want to interfere in that because you and your wife's split matters to her. Since I met Amarie, she's always talked highly about you. You have a chance with her. You just have to take it. My dad has a chain of restaurants and each one she's been to so far, she's enjoyed. I'll tell you what. Call her right now and tell her to get dressed." I quickly thought of how surprise dates always made her happy.

"My dad has a place called Fine Wine and Foods that she's been dying to try. Don't worry about anything. I have it," I told him.

"Now, I ain't balling like you, son, but I ain't hurting. I'm going to call her and tell her to be ready," he said as he looked at his phone screen.

Calling out to Siri, I had it call my dad's restaurant.

"Fine Wine and Foods. This is Marietta speaking. How may I help you?" She spoke.

"I need a reservation for let's say, four pm," I said.

"I'm sorry, but we are full for that time," she responded.

"This is Kasha, Ms. Marietta," I let her know.

"Oh, okay, I'm sorry. See you at four." She quickly changed her response before ending the call.

I noticed that Aaron had yet to call Amarie, and I wondered

why. I had been driving for about twenty minutes before I pulled up to his house. His face was filled with concern, and he looked flushed.

"She's not going to tell you no, especially when food is involved."

He let out a deep breath before pressing the call button.

"Hey umm, Amarie. This your dad," he started.

I could hear her laugh since he had the phone on speaker. I never knew why old people talked on speaker phone versus placing the phone to their ear.

"Dad, I know who you are. Are you okay? What's up?" she asked.

"Umm, yeah, I was wondering if umm, you would like to go out to eat with me. I'm with Kash right now, and he offered to drive us if you're okay with that. You know I can't drive right now, or I would." He started to just talk.

"Yeah, sure. Tell him I'm at the house that he has yet to bring me to," she said, and I knew exactly where she was.

Emily's big mouth ass must have told her about the house because she had taken her shopping earlier for me, while I handled my business. Emily could have gone on her own, but she knew if an adult went with her, chances are she wouldn't spend her own money. I did the smart thing and sent Amarie with her and only gave her a few thousand to spend on herself. I needed Emily to understand what it was like to spend her own money and get the feel of it. She had earned that two thousand dollars from me, and I knew she would also see that two thousand dollars could go further than she thought.

Amarie loved to shop, but she wasn't really into designer. She would rather go inside of PINK and Forever Twenty-One to spend money, which was how she always came out with so many bags. Instead of buying Gucci shoes and other top designers, she got Jordans and cheaper shoes. Emily would see that you didn't have to go all out to be cute. She often commented on how cute Amarie dressed, and I wondered if she would have the same opinion when she saw that it wasn't all designer. Now, granted, she owned some designer stuff but not as much as she could have.

"I love you, baby. I meant to take you the other day, but you know what happened," I shouted.

"It's okay. I love it, and I don't plan on going back home. Emily gave me my key," she told me.

"It's yours Ma. If you don't want to go back home, you don't have to. That's your house. I had my dad purchase it, and my mom and Emily decorate." I glanced over at the phone, wishing I could see the smile that I knew was on her face.

"I love you, daddy," she said.

"I love you too," Mr. Aaron and I said in unison.

He looked over at me just as the phone beeped, indicating that she had hung up.

"Ayee, man, now if she says daddy while I'm around, can you just let me have that?" he asked.

"I mean, she calls you dad, not daddy. I'm daddy." I laughed as he looked at me with a mean mug.

"I done had enough of your shit." He got out of the car to go and get dressed.

I rolled my weed and leaned my chair back to smoke as I watched a video that Amarie sent me of her going through the house. It was a single family six bedroom four-and-a-half-bathroom house. My favorite part was the back patio that had steps leading down to an even bigger backyard with a pool. Amarie loved to swim, and I knew she would put the pool to great use. She ran around the house like a big ass kid, making me want to go home and join her.

"I'm ready," her dad said as he climbed back into the car. He had gone from his Champion sweatsuit to a pair of tan slacks and a white button-down shirt. It was then that I noticed he had his cane.

"My right leg bothers me sometimes, and when it does, I use my cane. Usually, I can do some moving around without it," he told me.

"Oh, okay. You cleaned up nice, old school."

I pulled off and headed toward the restaurant. Our new house was about a forty-five-minute drive, which was why I had texted Amarie and told her to meet us there. If I went anywhere near the house, my ass was going to take a nap.

When I reached the restaurant, I pulled in behind Amarie's car. My baby stepped out, looking good as hell. Her jeans looked like they were painted on. She had on a cute blouse and some red bottom shoes. Walking over to her, I pulled her in for a kiss.

"You look beautiful, Ma. Go ahead and have fun. I'm going home and going to sleep. I'll be at the new house," I told her before walking over and giving her dad a manly hug. "Aye, old school, take care of daddy's girl," I joked before getting in my car and pulling off.

CHAPTER SEVENTEEN

VON

She was serious.

Natalie kept saying she was going to leave me alone, and I was starting to feel it. She hadn't asked me to come over since the last time I was over there, and that was a few days ago. I watched her Instagram, and she was back to being out all the time, while I was in the house bored and missing her. She knew she was bad in every way, and niggas fell at her feet. I knew she was being smart by constantly posting pictures with subliminal captions that had a flock of niggas commenting how they would treat her right.

When she texted me an hour ago to come pick my things up that I had mentioned needing as a way to come over, I didn't expect her to calmly respond with her location for me to come grab her key and get it. I guess she wasn't stopping her fun to accommodate me. A few days ago, I had asked Nakari to print me some pictures, and she did. I was glad I still had them in my car because they were going to come in handy.

Cousin in Law: *Could you grab me some edible fruit shit?*

Have it sent to Natalia's house but don't tell her. I'm sending money over now.

I sent her two hundred dollars on CashApp, and she quickly sent me a picture of the bouquet, saying they had to be picked up and that she would be able to bring them in an hour, which was fine with me.

I took my time driving to Natalia, and when I pulled up on her, of course she looked good as hell.

"So, you out here just doing you, huh?" I asked.

"That's what you wanted, right? I asked you what you were on, and you weren't ready for me, so what you expect?"

I nodded at her, then she strutted over to her car and climbed in. Once she was inside, she handed me the extra key to her house and then pulled off.

Shaking my head, I walked over to my car and climbed in. I drove to her house, and once I arrived, I went in my trunk, grabbed all my stuff, and dropped her gifts on the couch in the living room. Then I went back outside when Amarie called me and got the fruit from her.

"Thanks, cousin."

"You better snatch her up, and fast." She laughed before walking back to her car.

I closed the door behind me and got to work.

After grabbing all the candles that I brought, I made a path from the front door all the way to her bedroom. Going back, I lit every candle and then went back into her bedroom to grab one of the outfits and one of the sprays I had purchased for her from the Victoria Secret store, which I saw that all her panties were from. I also grabbed the rose petals and spread them from the front door to the bedroom, where I did my best to make a heart in the middle of the bed.

I grabbed the pictures Nakari had printed out for me and started to tape them from the strings of the balloons like I saw on Instagram. Finally, I went into the bathroom to take a quick twenty-minute shower, making sure I shaved and was completely clean. *Look at me acting like a bitch.* I laughed at myself.

Finally, I stepped out and quickly dried off, lotioning my body before I wrapped a towel around my waist. This was as good as it was going to get. I slid my socks on my feet and I placed some of the edible stuff Amarie had gotten for me on the bed.

I heard the front door open and went into the bathroom, closing the door.

"Oh shit, and this nigga trying to act like he ain't falling for a bitch," I heard her say as she came up the stairs.

Once I heard the bedroom door open, I came out.

"God damn, baby." Natalia smirked at me. "You really did your big one, daddy." She began to take her clothes off.

I bit my bottom lip and walked over to her as she dropped her bra on the floor. Just then, I heard barking from inside the closet. I had forgotten that I put the damn puppy inside the bag. I was glad it had them little air holes on the side, or the dog would have been dead.

Running into the closet I grabbed the bag and handed it to her. Natalia took the bag and quickly unzipped it. She gasped when she saw the small, shivering puppy hidden inside.

"Oh, my god! Daddy, you got us a puppy??" she squealed as she turned and picked up the gray and white puppy with blue eyes.

Looking between its legs, she moved the puppy around before she confirmed what I already knew, which was that the puppy was a girl.

"Man, fuck that dog. I'm trying to chill with you," I said, taking the puppy out of her hands and placing it in the hall before shutting the door.

"Can we name the puppy? Or you want to wait?" Natalia giggled as I placed kisses on her neck while backing her up to the bed.

Once she fell, I fell on top of her and spread her legs.

"I don't care. She's yours. You can name the damn thing whatever you want," I said as I picked her up.

Natalia wrapped her legs around my waist as I laid her back on the bed, kissing her from her neck down.

Once I reached her chest, I removed her bra and flicked my tongue across her nipples, causing a low moan to leave her lips. I worked my tongue down, tracing her panties before pulling them off and placing her legs on my shoulders. She had managed to take everything off except her panties. I placed soft kisses on her inner thighs before diving in.

"Mmm." Natalia moaned as I sucked lightly on her clit, making her body jerk. She quickly unwrapped her legs and sat up.

"You want to stop?" I asked, confused.

For a second, I was scared that I had hurt her in some way or that she really didn't want to fuck with me no more. Natalia shook her head no and pushed me, so I lay back.

She looked me in the eyes before she climbed on my lap and slowly kissed from my neck down. Her tongue traced my nicely cut six pack and the V-line that I took pride in. She pulled my towel off before grabbing my tool and licked it from the head to the base, causing me to groan.

She twirled her tongue around the head and then licked the little drip of pre cum off before she placed me in her mouth. Bobbing her head and working her hands on the part that she couldn't get into her mouth, she earned some loud groans from me with the work she was putting in. She sucked and pulled me out of her mouth, making the popping noise before she sucked me back in, only this time, relaxing her throat and deep throating me.

She tensed up a little as I began to pump in and out of her mouth, causing her to gag. My nut was right there, and I wasn't sure how she felt about swallowing, so I pulled her off me.

"If you want to swallow my nut, then keep going, but if not, I suggest you stop," I grunted.

She kept going, and like I said would happen, I let a loud growl come from my mouth as my babies shot down her throat. Natalia was a throat goat in my eyes because the girl kept sucking until I was fully hard again. I laid her back while placing myself at her entrance.

"Aww fuck!" Natalia screamed as I slid inside her.

I stayed still just enough for her to get used to my size like I always did. However, this time was so I didn't bust too fast. I wrapped her legs around my neck, pulling her close to me, and began to slow stroke her.

For some reason, I couldn't just fuck Natalia, not this time. Thoughts of her leaving me alone like she kept saying she would had me fucked up. I was ready to cut my hoes off and be just for her. I couldn't find myself saying it, so I was trying to show her.

Natalia moaned as I took my time.

"Faster, daddyyy," she cried in my ear.

I picked up the pace of my strokes, making her scream even louder. She sounded like I was killing her when I was only trying to murder the pussy. I unlocked her legs from around my neck and placed them on my shoulders as I stroked her a little rougher. Pulling my dick almost all the way out and then slamming it back in. I kept her that way for a good ten minutes before I let her climb on top of me.

My baby slid down slowly on me and began to rotate her

hips slow and then fast. I grabbed her waist and matched her strokes by slamming upwards into her. Her moans became uncontrollable, and I felt her body tense like it always did when she was about to cum.

My strokes stayed the same as I rubbed her pearl. "Ohhhh," she moaned as she came all over my dick and fingers.

I didn't stop, which only made Natalia body shake, and she began to squirt all over the place.

"Turn over. We not done yet." I slapped her thigh as she slowly turned over.

"Arch ya back."

Natalia got on all fours and arched her back. I smirked, loving that she was already a professional, and I didn't have to coach her. The way her ass spread when she tooted it in the air made me lick my lips.

"Damn, baby, you got to promise not to let nobody else but me hit this shit, okay?" I said.

Just like I thought, she didn't answer me; she only laughed. So, I unexpectedly slid into her, causing her to scream. My strokes were rough, deep, and hard. My hands rested in her hair as I pulled it.

"You promise baby, huh?" I harshly whispered. I was gon' make her ass promise me one way or another.

Natalia moaned loudly and nodded. That only made me get rougher. I wanted her to say it out loud and mean it.

"Say it, then. Let a nigga take care of you. Teach me how to love," I said as I slapped her ass and pulled her hair, slamming into her harder.

Natalia let a tear slip, and she tried to wipe it away, but I knocked her hand down.

"Javonnn, baby you hurting my stomach." She moaned as she began to squirt out of nowhere.

"Von... shittttt." She moaned louder.

"Shut up and take this dick" I grunted, only picking up the pace.

The only sounds were Natalia's loud ass moans and our skin slapping. I was sure the neighbors knew I gave out great dick by now.

Crack- Crack-boom

"Javon, I promise. I promise, and you just broke my bed," Natalia let me know.

"Mmm shit!" I hollered as I began to pump as fast as I could.

I pushed Natalia's face into the pillow to muffle her screams. The way she sounded, I was scared the neighbors would call the police as I busted my nut all over her back and ass.

"Damn, I'll get you a new bed frame in the morning. My bad, ma," I said as I grabbed some baby wipes and wiped my kids off her back and ass before placing them in the trash can on the side of the bed.

Natalia watched me before she turned her back, and light snores filled the room. I lay next to her, hoping I was making the right moves with my life.

CHAPTER EIGHTEEN

NAKARI

I sat on my living room floor, just staring at the empty space, trying to find something else to clean. It was the only way I could deal with life. Everything for everybody seemed to come together, while my life was falling apart, and no one seemed to notice.

Hearing the front door unlock, I didn't move. I really didn't care who it was. I continued to look for any little thing that was out of place.

"Bestie, you good? Why the hell are you sitting in here with cleaning supplies and nothing to clean. And why do you have a pile of money?" Amarie grabbed me by the chin and lifted my head.

I inhaled then exhaled, trying to find the right words to say to her, but she went on.

"And why the hell it smells like bleach and Lysol in here? You done shined every ounce of this damn house. Where's the furniture?" she questioned.

"It was old, and I wanted something new, so I got some

new furniture. It'll be here tomorrow, so I have time to deep clean my house," I muttered.

"What's up, ma? Talk to me. You haven't been at work. You look like death smacked you in the face, and the house is so empty it looks like you just moved in. Let me be here for you." Amarie sighed as she sat on the floor with me.

"I couldn't care less about what I look like or that job. I can always find new employment," I spoke barely above a whisper.

"But why?"

"What do you mean why? You don't see what's happening to me? My once happy life is fucked up. I'm watching everyone live, and honestly, I don't know how to be around everyone. I feel fucked up for being upset over Capri. It just keeps going back to her, and she was doing me wrong the whole time. I want to move on, but I'm afraid of what the next person might do," I admitted.

"Moving on may be what you need. You know they say the best way to get over someone is with someone else. You're looking for love, and that's why you haven't found it. Look at Von and Natalia, or me for example. Shit just fell on us. We wasn't trying to be in it. What's for you gon' be for you. The right person is waiting for you. Y'all just not ready for each other yet," Amarie said.

It sounded good, but that was it. Everything sounded good, but nothing made me feel better.

"I don't want to be here anymore, and not just because of this thing with Capri. I'm just overwhelmed by life. I feel like I'm not making any progress, and I often have these moments where my heart is racing, and I feel like I can't breathe. I just want it to stop. It's like my mind is playing tricks on me." I tried to explain the feelings I'd been having. Since things started happening around us, everything for me seemed so hard.

I wasn't sure how to deal with things because I never really had to. My mom was always there to pick up the pieces, which was why I knew if anything ever happened to her, I would be lost.

"I'm here if you need me. Don't ever forget that. I don't feel too good, so I'm going to go home and lay down. I don't care if you just need to talk. Call my phone, and we can stay on the phone until you don't want to anymore, and if you need me to come over, just say so, and I will. I know how you get, and I know you want to be left alone. Please, just don't do anything crazy. Try smoking and taking a nap." Amarie got off the floor, kissed me on the cheek, let me know she loved me, and left.

Standing up, I wiped everything down again before walking up my stairs to the bathroom to start my shower. I washed my body twice before throwing on some jeans and a shirt. I grabbed my bottle of Hennessy and my weed, then went to Penn Treaty Park to sit by the water.

The entire drive there, I didn't play any music. I focused on the drive the whole time. Every now and then, I would place my finger on my neck to make sure I still had a pulse or even roll my window down because I felt like I was suffocating. Being the person that I was, I had googled my symptoms and diagnosed myself with anxiety and panic attacks. I also may have had a mild heart attack due to the chest pain.

Getting out of my car, I walked over to the water and took a seat. I took a few swigs of the Hennessy while rolling my weed.

"How you been?" DeJuan appeared out of nowhere, scaring the hell out of me.

"I've been good. Thanks for asking." I looked around, trying to figure out where he had come from.

"That's good." His eyes were glossy, and I could tell he was high.

I almost wondered how it felt to be high because addicts

never really cared what was going on when they were high, and anything would feel better than how I felt at that moment. Weed and alcohol didn't seem to help too much anymore, so I did both until I fell asleep.

"You sure you okay? You don't look like the girl you usually are. You seem down," he said, sparking his weed and puffing it.

He tried to hand it to me, but I shook my head no. I had my own.

"I'm good. You mind leaving me alone? You hurt my cousin pretty bad, and I don't agree with that," I told him.

"I know I fucked up with her. I'm supposed to be in rehab right now, but I can't leave this shit alone. It makes me forget everything going on and just be at peace. Even if it's just for a few hours, it's better than suffering every day. You know I used to try to tell my mom I heard voices and that I wanted to kill myself. Nobody listened until I actually started trying to take myself out. One day my dad left his drugs in his office, and I tried some. At first, I could control it. I only did it to silence the voices in my head, but it soon got out of control. Some people can function, while it took complete control of my life," he shared.

When he stood to leave, a bag fell from his pocket. I knew I should have stopped him and told him, but I didn't. Instead, I picked it up and twirled it between my fingers. Placing it back down, I began to roll my weed. As I looked around, I noticed DeJuan had walked off and was climbing into his car. Picking the bag up, I figured it wouldn't hurt to try just a little of it to see if it really made my problems go away. After sprinkling a little in my weed, I finished rolling before lighting it.

"What could it hurt?" I said to myself before placing the blunt to my lips.

My stomach twisted from my nerves, yet I still decided to take a pull. I started coughing before I took another pull.

The kind of rush that ran through my body had me leaning my head back and smiling. Everything I'd just felt went away. My heart was racing, though, and my mouth was dry. Grabbing the bottle of Henny, I took a swig.

"Hey, relax. You good." DeJuan's voice filled the air as I grabbed my chest.

My heart was beating so fast that I thought it would beat out of my chest.

"Enjoy the feeling. You're alright." He shook me by my arm.

"I just need to breathe. I got to catch my breath," I said, but it felt like my breathing was going so slowly.

"Relax. Let me make you feel better." He tapped his cold hand on my thigh.

"No, I'm good. You dropped that on purpose?" I asked, and he smirked.

"You're taking the fun out of this. You know I wanted you, and I told you I would get you. You always had something to say about me being a crackhead, and now look at you," he said, holding my cheeks and blowing smoke in my face. He was smoking from a crack pipe, and it was hard to not breathe it in.

After a while, my heart wasn't beating fast anymore, and my whole body relaxed. DeJuan was still there, but he was quiet. He looked over at me and slid his hand into the slit of my jeans. Someone touching me so gently made my body feel good. I didn't know if it was the high, but his touch was driving me crazy.

I looked away and blinked, thinking this wasn't real. But when DeJuan eased my pants down, and I didn't stop him, I knew it was. The feelings he gave me overpowered what I knew was right, and that was to get the fuck away from him.

"Here." He handed me my weed back, and I took another pull. This time, I didn't cough.

DeJuan tossed my legs over his shoulders and let his tongue swipe across my neatly shaved box.

"Oh, god." My body jerked.

I arched my back and kept DeJuan's head steady by pulling on his hair. I rode his face to the sound of the waves crashing against the rocks.

"Don't stop... Oh goooooodddddd, please don't stop!" I cried, grinding into his face harder.

I could feel him muttering something, but the vibration of his voice only added to the intensity. I didn't give a damn what he had to say or who saw us in the moment. The high I was on, I didn't want to come down from.

I'll ask him what he said later, I thought. DeJuan stuck his tongue inside me and flicked it lightly, just enough to drive me crazy. He knew exactly where my spot was, and I didn't even know how he found it. Just when my legs began to shake, DeJuan took his tongue out and instead began to nibble gently on my clit.

"You gon' cum for daddy, ma?" DeJuan asked, his voice laced with lust.

He chuckled when my eyes, which were shut tight enough to be screwed together, opened. I nodded before pushing his head back between my legs. I didn't need to look in his face; it would only remind me of the fucked up shit I was doing. DeJuan lifted my legs and licked down to the crack of my ass then back up.

"Yeah. Yes, I'm going to... awwwww shit!" I cried when he attached his mouth back to me and slurped.

I couldn't even remember what I was going to say. All the words in my head flew out when a feeling so strong and intense hit me. My legs began to shake, and a feeling of euphoria took over. The way my body was locked up and jerking, I felt like I was in a scary movie and a demon was trying to come out of me.

DeJuan let me up with a smile on his face. I didn't care what he said or did next; I was in a great mood, and I didn't want to come down off it. So, when he told me he would see me soon and walked off, I didn't bother to say anything.

No matter how high I was or how he had just made my body feel, I vowed to steer clear of DeJuan and his drugs and take this shit to the grave. It was a vow I would do anything to keep.

CHAPTER NINETEEN

NATALIA

"Come on. You really gon' take your clothes off for some random niggas? What the hell you got to strip for? We ain't broke or hurting for money. Your ass been saying you wanted to do this for God knows how long, and you choose now? And where the hell is Nakari to help me talk you out of this?" Amarie said, like I was going to change my mind.

The thrill of dancing in a room full of niggas was on my bucket list, and I had to cross it off since Javon and I seemed to be making moves in the right direction.

I stepped out of the car, making sure to put an extra sway in my hips. The six-inch red bottoms added to my look. Running my hand through my big curls, I was about to tear the stage the fuck up and have these niggas digging deep in their pockets. Twirling in front of the car window, I chuckled at the look on Amarie's face.

She certainly didn't look like she wanted to be there with me. However, who else was going to cheer me on while I did dumb shit? With a white bodycon dress and a blue jean jacket on, it would be a lie to say a bitch like me wasn't the shit.

Walking into the club, I hid all my nervousness as I switched my hips. Knowing I had every male's attention in the room, I strutted over to the bar.

This is going to be quick and easy, I thought as I waited quietly until the bartender, a caramel-skinned girl with natural curls, got to me.

"What can I get for you?" the mid-twenties aged woman politely asked while wiping down the bar.

"I spoke to the owner earlier, and we set up an interview for four. I know I'm a little early, but can you let him know I'm here?" I explained, barely able to hear myself over the speakers.

All that hot girl shit I was just outside kicking to Amarie was slowly leaving my body, and I knew I needed a shot before I completely backed out.

"Actually, he's not here right now. He won't be back for a couple of hours. However, I'm the hiring manager. What's your name? Natalia, right?" She smiled,

Usually, I wouldn't trust a female, but I sensed no negative energy coming from the bartender.

"Yeah," I answered.

"I'm Trina, nice to meet you." She extended her hand.

Amarie's ass sat quietly the whole time with a look of disgust on her face. I knew her ass was plain sick of me and my antics, but she always had my back.

"Umm... okay. Am I being interviewed right here?" I questioned.

I knew I'd have to show my body soon, but I hoped that I would be able to keep some clothes on and still make a bunch of money. My first and last time up there would hopefully be at any moment other than that one.

"No, girl. In my office. Can you do a working interview?" Trina rushed, ushering me into the back of the club.

Passing all the lockers and the intimidating stares of the other strippers, I kept my head up and listened intently to what she said. "Basically, it's what we call a practice round, but for business purposes, we call it a working interview. Now, I hear you only want to do it this once, so I'm going to let you. You'll give us a song, we'll send you up there and see how they respond to you. It's all about what the customers like, so if you get good feedback, I can tell you that Manny will let you come back and work his club whenever you want," Trina explained before giving Amarie a bag that had a big dollar sign on the front. I guessed it was for my money.

"This is your interview, so we prepare you, but after this, if you get the job, you're required to bring your own clothes and props. Understood?"

"Heard you, even though I won't be working here. I just wanted to cross this shit off my bucket list," I softly said.

"You have exactly thirty-five minutes until you're up," Trina announced.

Once we were sure the coast was clear, Amarie and I looked at each other, and I let all the fake confidence out in one breath.

"Girl, my ass is scared as hell," I admitted.

"You got this. You got my ass in here in the back of this club that smells like ass and underarms, so now you got to go up there. And you better do your big one since you got all the nappy wig wearing bitches staring at me," Amarie hyped me up.

After touching up my curls and applying one coat of clear lip gloss, I struggled into the corseted one piece. Once I made sure I had put everything on right, I had to accept the obvious —the outfit was clearly made for someone who didn't have curves like me, and I was too thick for it. Amarie grabbed the scissors and cut a slit under the arms and on the thighs to give me room to breathe. I knew damn well I should have brought a bigger size; this was going to be something we forever talked about.

"You ready? Oh. My. Damn. Girl, you were born for this. You're the first person who's actually worked an outfit like that. I mean, it looks like you can't breathe, but it's definitely giving what it's supposed to give. They're going to love you. What you want us to call you?" Trina giggled as she walked up to fix a runaway piece of string that Amarie had clearly left.

"Storm, because it was storming when I thought of this shit. Yup, Storm is fine," I said.

Amarie nodded in agreement.

"This is for you. Drink fast. It'll help." Trina handed me a drink, but I handed it back.

"I don't drink nothing I ain't see being poured. Thank you, though," I whispered, as if there was someone else in the room besides Amarie. I didn't want to offend her, but that was something I lived by.

After pouring up three shot glasses, Trina passed them around. I noticed that Amarie didn't throw her shot back like she usually would. Instead, she handed it to me. I looked at her with a raised brow.

"I need to be sober for this shit." She shrugged,

After tossing back both shots, I poured a few more and shrugged too. Trina ushered us both out of the room and close to the stage.

"Oh, wait... what song do you want the DJ to play?" she stopped and asked, pulling me back before she went on the stage.

After thinking about it for a moment, I whispered the name of the song in Trina's ear, making her look me up and down.

"Yeah, you're going to be a money maker, for sure. I can already tell." She laughed and patted me on the back before going to the DJ booth.

Taking a deep breath before stepping onto the stage, I closed my eyes and listened to the DJ to announce me. "PLEASE GIVE IT UP FOR OUR FRESH MEAT! Now, don't be stingy. This is her first and only dance, so, fellas, help me welcome Storm to the stage!" the DJ yelled, hyping up the crowd.

But all the hype in the world couldn't prepare any of the guys in there for the show I was about to put on. Tying my black satin robe tighter around my waist, I walked up against the pole and posed. I made sure I bent over like Latto had done in her pictures, with her hand between her legs, covering her box.

Now we're sitting at the table, sipping the finest wine
Having a damn good time, I know what's on your mind
I want you, you want me too
Stop fronting, I know exactly what you want, you want to
Do it to me, I wanna feel you touch my body, baby, body, baby
Do it to me, I guarantee you won't regret it
Let me set it out like you ain't never had it
Do it to me, I want you to grab me, talk to me
Tell me how you like it, when you want it, when you all up on it
Do it to me, I'm gonna give it to you
I'm gonna make this a night to remember

Usher's "Do It To Me" blared through the speakers as I performed tricks that I had never done before.

I slowly climbed to the top of the pole and flipped my body upside down, then grinded on the pole as I slowly made my way down. Before I reached the bottom, I spread both my legs wide open and locked eyes with my man. I wanted to let go and run off stage, but it was too late. The fire that danced in his eyes made me look away.

I flipped myself over and landed in a split. Then I slowly sat up on my knees and rotated my hips while traveling my hands down my body. Bending over, I arched my back and slowly crawled across the stage before lying down and doing the crybaby dance but in a sexy way, making sure my ass jiggled every time I hit the floor. Rolling over, I bent one of my legs while the other lay flat and arched my body up. Then I slowly stood and walked back over to the pole. I used my upper body strength to climb back up and flip my body, slowly walking across the ceiling. These were all things I did at home. Loosening my arm, I did flips all the way down the pole, landing on the ground in a straddle just as the lights cut off.

Once the music ended, my heart rate slowed down until I saw the piles of money on the floor.

"That high is something else," I told Amarie as she helped me collect the money. Her ass was picking up money so fast that I had to stop and laugh.

"Kash gon' kill me. Bitch, I told him I was sick and couldn't make it into the office earlier today, and now here I am in the club, entertaining you. You better pick my head up if he knocks it off," she said, and my mouth dropped.

"You still don't feel good, do you? Your ass ain't drink, and you look like you about to throw up," I said as I got back to picking up the money.

Trina came over once we were done and walked us to Manny's office. After shutting and locking the office door, she walked over to the money counter, and we placed all the money in the machine. After about three minutes, she whistled.

"Girl, you made five thousand tonight," Trina said in astonishment.

"Whatttt?" I looked over at the counter.

Had I known I could make money like that, I would have been got up on that stage.

"Manny usually takes a cut, but he asked me not to get it from you. He also asked me to bring you both to his office because someone is here," she started just as the door flew open.

"Baby, I was just here to support my cousin." Amarie sold me out as soon as Kash came through the door, followed by a very angry Javon.

"So, this what we doing, right? Shaking your ass for money? You out here like you belong on that stage. You should only be doing that shit for me!" Javon shouted.

"I didn't shake my ass. I was being an exotic dancer, and I didn't take my clothes off," I replied with just as much attitude.

"Bet. I see what the fuck you on. You want me to treat you like one of these stripper bitches too, Ms. exotic dancer of the fucking night?" Javon was now in my face, and the spit flying from his mouth was making me mad.

"Look, I'm sorry. It was just something I wanted to do, and I wanted to get it out of the way. That doesn't mean I don't respect you as my man."

"Bitch, you don't, because my woman would never be out here swinging on poles," he said before walking out of the room and taking my heart with him.

CHAPTER TWENTY
AMARIE

S itting up from the couch, my body shivered. It felt like someone had placed my body in an ice bath for the time that I had been asleep. Hearing Kash unlock the door, I lay back down and pulled the blanket tighter around me. I was freezing cold and didn't know what kind of sickness I had.

Kash walked over and sat on the edge of the couch. He pushed my hair back, causing my wig to slide off. I guess I had sweated out the glue.

"My bad. I was trying to get the hair off your face." He frowned when he felt my forehead. "Amarie, you're sick. You're burning up, and you need to go to the hospital," he said while watching me shiver.

Kasha grabbed my hands in his. "Your hands are cold."

I slapped his hand away.

"Come on we're going to the hospital. Okay?" he ordered, even though he made it sound like I had an option.

He helped me sit up, causing a sharp pain in my head. The

headache had been there all day but not as bad. It came and went but now had returned full force.

"Ma, what's wrong?" Kash was concerned.

I was sure it was because I had gone from sitting up to being doubled over. I lay back down and placed the blanket over my face to block out the light.

Kash pulled out a bottle of Tylenol and handed it to me with a bottle of ice-cold water from the refrigerator. I tossed two pills in my mouth and slowly stood. We made our way out the door, and right before we got to the car, my head felt like it was spinning.

"You cool? What's wrong?" Kash grabbed me just as I closed my eyes.

It felt like my body was giving out on me. I tried to grab onto the car, but everything went black.

———

Waking up to beeping machines, I struggled to open my eyes.

"How are you feeling? You gave your husband quite a scare, I hear." The doctor chuckled.

I remembered walking to the car but nothing after that, and the word husband was really confusing to hear. I knew I wasn't out for that long, or was I?

Sitting up in bed, I glanced out into the hallway and saw Javon talking to Kash, who was sitting down with his head in his hands.

The thought of him calling me his wife usually would've made me excited, but my head was throbbing too much to really care.

"Sorry, umm... Can I go now? I feel fine," I lied, attempting to pull the IV from my hand.

"Were you aware that you're about nine weeks pregnant?"

the doctor asked, writing on her clipboard as she sat on the stool.

My mouth immediately went dry, and the dizziness came back.

"Wh... what? How is that possible? I mean, I know how it's possible, but I'm on birth control!" I cried, silencing myself when I remembered that Kash was right in the hallway. Thinking about what he would say when I told him I had been forgetting my pills sometimes, I began to cry.

"Well, there are options. However, I will suggest that if you decide to continue your pregnancy, you need to take it easy. Your blood pressure was extremely high when you came in, which could be why you passed out. Also, you needed fluids. You may want to increase your water intake. I'll let you talk to your husband, and then, if you two want one, we'll get you an ultrasound. We want to make sure everything is okay with the fetus," the doctor explained.

When I nodded in understanding, she left the room, stopping to talk to Kash for only a second. When I saw both Kash and the Javon look into the room at me, I dropped my head, pretending that I wasn't trying to imagine what their conversation sounded like.

When Kash walked into the room and shut the door, I continued to stare at my fingers as if there was something new about my white nail polish.

"How you feeling'?" he asked, sitting at the edge of the bed.

As soon as he spoke those words, tears welled in my eyes. He scooted closer to me in alarm.

"What's wrong, ma? You got Covid or sum?" he joked, trying to get me to smile, except all it did was turn my crying into a full-blown sob. I wished it was as simple as Covid. Hell, anything besides a baby.

"Kash, I'm so sorry. I was taking my pills. I swear I was! I'm usually good with them, but I don't know what happened!" I cried louder, making him stand up.

"The doctor said come talk to you, but your ass in here talking about pills and shit. Is this a code or something? What the fuck is wrong?" he questioned louder while pacing the floor.

"I'm... I'm pregnant." I hiccupped and covered my face with my hands.

The room fell silent, and Javon's ass was in the doorway with his mouth wide open. When I looked away from his ass and at Kash, he was in the corner, staring at me with a small smile on his face.

"How far along are you?" he quietly asked, looking in every direction but mine.

"The doctor said about nine weeks... Kasha, I can't do this. How I'm supposed to do this when you said a year? I didn't try to trap you, I swear to God!" I cried, subconsciously placing my hand on my stomach.

After about five minutes of silence, Javon walked into the room. He probably couldn't take listening from outside no more.

"You are not alone this time, ma. I been said I had you, and if we are being honest, I knew what was going to happen. I threw your pills out the day you got them and brought them to my house. You never mentioned it, and neither did I. So, if anything, I trapped you. Whatever you tell this doctor when she comes back, I hope you consider how I feel. I want to be a dad, and I want a family with you. Don't make an irrational decision. Please don't take my child away from me. Please, I'll do anything," Kash begged with tears coming from his eyes.

I knew then that the decision was made. We would have to figure this out because my ass was having his baby.

"So, I'm having a godson? 'Cause I know this baby was

made out of love. I think guys who ain't really ready for a child and out here being a hoe always get daughters. You know, like how I used to be. I think God gives them to us to try and humble us, just because it ain't no way I would want a nigga to be out here doing my baby how I was doing these females," Von said.

"Bro, who even told you to come? I mean, I'm thankful you pulled up, but come on now. Your ass is too much. Like who even said our child was having a godparent, and even if they did, who said it would be you?" I asked.

"Man, tell her she got the game fucked up. That's all our baby. I'm gon' be at all the appointments too. I just will stay in the hall when it's time for them to do all the extra shit. We in the game now. In fifteen years, I'm gon' have my own child, so this one can babysit. I can see me and Natalia now, well after she get her shit together. We still going to be trying to party. I need a legit babysitter, so y'all can come out to party." Von's ass was serious, and that's what made it funny.

The doctor walked back in with a smile on her face.

"It looks like you all talked. So, what did we decide? Just so I can give you proper treatment and prescriptions." She waited for me to answer but Von spoke up instead.

"I'm about to be the best uncle the world has ever seen. So, yeah, we keeping it." He dapped Kash up.

The doctor laughed before she wrote some more things on her clipboard.

"Can I have something for my head?" I asked.

"Yes. Someone will bring in some pain meds in a second. I want to keep you overnight, just to monitor you and the baby and make sure your blood pressure goes down," she said before walking back out.

"Javon, Natalia said she on her way home and for you to meet her there," I lied, thinking it would make him leave.

Instead, his always angry ass pulled his phone out. He tapped on the screen a few times before Natalia's voice filled the room.

"I'm on my way." She hung up, and I knew that meant she was on her way to the hospital.

I knew if Natalia was coming, everyone was coming with her, and I would have to break the news that I was carrying a baby. I wanted to let everyone know at the same time, and it wasn't now.

"Don't go running y'all mouths. I want to tell everyone at the same time."

Within an hour, my room was full of people asking me what was going on. I told them all the same thing. I had high blood pressure and didn't know. I even had Kash go out and tell the doctor not to mention the baby. I knew my family would want to be involved as much as they could, and I wanted Kash's family to have that very same opportunity.

The nurse came and told everyone they had to leave, and that visiting hours were over. Of course, Kash stayed by my side until they released me the next morning.

"Make sure you follow up with prenatal care," the doctor told me as she handed over my discharge papers.

I agreed with her and smiled. I was headed home to my own bed after being in that hard ass bed, freezing all night. Hospitals gave you those thin ass blankets in hopes of keeping you warm, but they didn't do it for me. Kash was quiet the whole drive home, and I wondered what thoughts consumed his mind.

"What you are thinking about?" I asked as we kicked our shoes off by the front door.

"I'm going to be a dad in a matter of months. I'm thinking of how I have someone to pass down everything I own. I'm thinking of how the girl of my dreams is carrying my child. I'm thinking that we are making the right decisions in life, because with all that's going on, God has blessed me in the most beautiful way. The two things I was missing in my life are now right here in front of me." He placed his hands on my flat stomach.

Had the doctors not told me I was pregnant, I would never have known. I prayed that all the drinking and everything else I had done didn't mess with my baby's health. Just like Kash had all those thoughts, I did too. Sometimes I felt like things were moving fast, and other times I felt like things were not moving at all. However, things with us weren't planned; everything just happened, and I embraced every moment. I knew I was about to experience the journey of giving life, and I was about to do that with the one who in my eyes was the best person to share it with. Kash always made sure I was okay, so I knew he would make sure his kid was good too. Kash was patient and caring; something I prayed he'd pass on to my child.

"I really love you. I don't just be telling you that." He kissed my forehead.

I knew he loved me. I felt it in all the things he did and spoke. I just hoped he felt my love for him too.

CHAPTER TWENTY-ONE

KASH

My baby was having my baby, and I was so excited about it. Amarie wanted to wait to tell everyone, but I was ready to tell the whole world. My mom and dad had only been gone a few days, and I knew she wanted to wait until they came back, but that was just too long for me.

"How about we tell my mom and dad since they just went back home? We can FaceTime them and let them know, and then we can do something special to let your family know. I'm excited as hell, and I know you don't want to share the news, but come on, ma," I said.

"Okay. Call your mom, and we can show her the paperwork. Or let's make a little slide show or something. I don't know," she nervously said.

I dialed my mom's number, and she immediately answered. Usually, my mom's beautiful face was smiling. However, today she wore a deep frown.

"Hey, son," my mom said to me.

"Hey, Ma. Amarie is right here as well," I stated.

"Hey, love. How are you all doing?"

"Good. We have some great news for you," I said and pointed the camera at Amarie, who was smiling hard.

"Umm, are you okay with being a grandmom?" she asked.

My mom jumped up, dropping the phone and screaming.

"Yes, Lord! Finally!" my mom yelled, and my dad could be heard asking what was wrong.

"Amarie is having a baby," I heard her say.

The phone was picked up, and my dad's face came on the screen.

"That's great, son. Good job." My dad smiled at us.

"Thank you," I replied.

We hung up with them and called everyone else. I knew Amarie wanted to do something big, but in my eyes, there was no point. Of course, she would have a crazy baby shower and an even better welcome home party. I was going all out and would even get her a push gift.

When we were done with all our calls, Amarie stood up from the couch and turned the TV on. When she looked over at me, she bit her lip. We were having a lot of sex nowadays, so much that I had to start googling new shit. She walked over and stripped me of my clothes. I stepped out of my jeans and let her push me back on the bed. Then, she climbed on top of me and kissed my lips. I wrapped my arms around her waist and squeezed her ass. I was always bringing myself back to the day when I wondered was it at as soft as it looked, and yes, it was.

She slowly slid her tongue into my mouth while keeping her eyes locked on mine. We let ourselves get lost in the kiss. Our tongues wrestled for dominance before I let her win. I moaned into her mouth as I let my hands go up and rub her breasts.

Amerie kissed me all over my face, letting her lips travel down my body. She kissed and sucked on my neck for a second then moved down to my chest. Her tongue twirled around one of my nipples while she lightly pinched the other.

"Do I make you feel good?" she asked.

I nodded, letting my moans give her the answer she was looking for. She switched her mouth to my other nipple before letting her tongue travel down my stomach, dip into my belly button, then meet the most sensitive spot on my body. Today, I let her have control because she often complained about how I never did. I wanted to make her happy, so I sat back and let her do all the work.

Amarie flicked her tongue across my dick, and I swore she might have been spelling her name or something with the different tricks she was doing. She sucked me into her mouth and then let her tongue slide back and forth across my dick.

"You not gon' ever get tired of me, are you? I know I be overly horny all the time."

"That's one thing I'm not worried about, and all you need to be worried about is the way I'm about to bless you with all this thickness," I decided to say.

Quickly changing my mind because she was doing too much talking, I picked her up and placed her on the top of the computer stand we had in the living room. I stepped between her legs, and she closed her eyes soon as she felt my lips travel across the side of her neck. I licked her neck before biting it and sucking hard. She let a low moan out of her mouth.

Grabbing my hand, she slid it inside her panties and let me do my thing. My fingers worked like magic if you let her tell it. She often referred to me as a DJ. I twirled her pearl between my index finger and thumb while sucking her nipples one at a time. I knew I was doing a good job when her head fell back. I decided to turn things up a bit, so I slid two fingers inside her wet tunnel and dug my way through. I pumped my fingers in and out, using my thumb to apply pressure to her clit. The way she bit down on my lip, I thought she was going to draw blood.

"You ready to feel this dick?" I asked. She nodded her head, too eager to talk. "Tell me. Tell daddy you want this dick," I begged. I loved her voice when we were having sex. It drove me crazy.

Amarie smiled before lowering her gaze. "Daddy, can you give me my dick, please?" she whispered in my ear before licking it, causing me to groan.

I lined my dick up, and without warning, slammed into her. I began to pump in and out. Each time I got inside her wet, tight, cave, it seemed like it was wetter than before. The gushy noise it made had me thinking of the time my car ran out of gas, and I was stuck on the side of the highway.

"Fuck," I damn near growled when she clenched her muscles around me. I knew my dick was deep inside her when she creamed all over me.

"That's right, baby. Let me feel my pussy cum," I told her before picking her up and bouncing her up and down on me like a pogo stick. I was in pure heaven, and I hoped she was there with me. If not, that was on her. "Place your leg on my shoulder," I said after placing her back on her feet.

She leaned back against the wall and lifted her leg. It looked like she was standing up in a full split. I had every access to the pussy that I wanted, and she allowed me to. I started to pound into her hard. I licked my thumb before reaching around and placing the tip of my thumb in her butt, sending her crazy.

"Baby, stop. I can't take no more!" she cried, but I wasn't trying to hear any of that.

Amarie was asking for dick, so I was giving it. She kept crying out how she couldn't take it. I let out a long sigh but ended up letting her leg down. She pushed me back and climbed on top of me.

Placing her hands on my ankles, my woman eased herself down on me and slowly came back up before dropping back down and rotating her hips. This girl could ride dick like a pro. Her ass jiggled each time she bounced, making me smack it.

She rocked in a circular motion, then back and forth. Amarie even leaned forward and bounced her ass on me hard as hell. I gripped her cheeks and fucked her back since she wanted to show off.

"Throw that ass on me, baby."

I smiled as my toes curled. She lifted herself up and began to bounce hard up and down on me while rubbing her own clit. My baby sent us both into a shaking fit as we came and nodded off.

———

Waking up to the sound of my alarm, I slid out of bed and headed to take a shower. Amarie was still fast asleep, and I didn't want to wake her. She said she needed to pay Nakari a visit later, and that was all she had to do, so I let her sleep.

I took my morning piss before stepping into the shower and letting the water run over my head. After washing my body and hair, I stepped out of the shower and wrapped a towel around me. I grabbed my toothbrush and brushed my teeth. Once I was done, I quietly went into the walk-in closet and slipped on a pair of Ethika boxers. Looking around, I decided to put on a pair of Amiri jeans and an Amiri shirt. I grabbed my Apple Watch and slipped my feet into my buttas, then headed downstairs to leave.

I double checked to make sure it was locked, and all the cameras were on. Deciding to switch my cars today, I walked over to my new Dodge Durango and hit the locks. I climbed in and drove to the barber shop. It had been a while since I'd gone to see my barber because lately, he had been coming to me.

I was early, so I knew no one had arrived. I walked into his shop and took a seat in his chair.

"What's good, my boy? I'm glad to see you out here and alive," he said.

"Yeah, you know I'm not going out that easy. What's up with you?" I asked as he dropped a cape around me.

"Shit, the lady 'bout to drop number five. I'm ready to get a vasectomy. I wanted a big family but not a damn soccer team. We both too fertile," he joked, and I had to agree.

Since Jason had his first child, every year he'd had another one. His kids were all back-to-back. His wife went from running a hair shop to just renting it out since she never had time to go back. Her ass stayed pregnant and wobbling around. I wanted a big family, but two to three kids would make it big. I wasn't trading my cars in for no damn soccer van.

"Where Von been? His ass is usually up in here twice a week. I haven't been seeing him," he said as he started to cut me.

"Shit, I'm surprised. You know his ass be everywhere, which is why I don't know why he ain't been in here. Then again, you know he booed up now, so that probably is a factor," I said.

"Hey, Kash, long time no see." Kacey, the shampoo girl, smiled when she walked in.

"What's up?" I simply stated.

Kacey used to suck my dick a whole lot back in the day before my girl came along. I wasn't with that no more, so I saw no reason for us to be in contact, not even for something as simple as getting my hair washed.

"Damn, that's what we on?" she replied with fake hurt.

"Hell yeah. My wife sucks dick way better," I let her know, so she could stop talking to me.

One thing I knew about a female was they didn't like to be compared to other females, especially if they were losing to them.

Once Jason finished, I paid him and dapped him up. It was time for me to go to the market and grab some food. Amarie could have done it, but I figured since I was out, and she wanted to spend time with her cousin, I could do it just to lighten her load.

CHAPTER TWENTY-TWO

DEJUAN

I walked ten minutes to the store and went inside. I was down to my last hundred dollars and badly needed food. A few months ago, nobody would have been able to tell me I would be sleeping outside and struggling to make ends meet. My family thought I was in rehab, but I was really bouncing from corner to corner downtown. A few people I met showed me how to get by. All I needed was a tent in a few blankets.

This wasn't the life I wanted to live, and the only thing that would help me was rehab. Before I got completely clean, I wanted to do one more thing, and that was hurt Amarie in a way that she would struggle to fix. That's why I dropped that baggie near Nakari. I knew she was weak; she had always been. She also was the one who always tried new stuff at parties, so I knew it would be pretty easy to get her hooked, just like it was for me. What I didn't expect was for her to let me eat her pussy.

Back in the day, Nakari hated my guts and couldn't stand me for her cousin. Hell, she didn't even look at me twice. And now, there I was, able to say I had done things to her that I never would have imagined. I knew Nakari would try to take this to the grave, which was why I had been blowing her up. I needed her to meet me, so I could record her while she did drugs and let me have my way with her.

I had a friend who worked at a rundown motel, and for twenty dollars, he would let me get one of the empty rooms. So, some nights when it rained, I would sleep there instead of on the streets. I knew he couldn't do it all the time, so I didn't try. I had Nakari's number because of Amarie, so getting in contact with her wasn't hard at all. I dialed her number, and she picked up.

"Stop calling my phone," she fussed.

"Just let me get you high and fuck you this time. Plus, I already have it on video. All I got to do is send it to Natalia or Amarie's phone," I lied.

She sucked her teeth but agreed to meet me. I continued through the aisle, grabbing myself a rag and a pair of boxers along with a pair of sweats and a shirt. I was homeless, but I wasn't dirty. This was my last time getting high, which was why I spent all the money I had. After I did what I needed to do with Nakari, I was going to check myself into rehab and start the process of getting my life together. I no longer wanted to live how I was living out there.

CHAPTER TWENTY-THREE

NAKARI

I pulled up to DeJuan's favorite motel and parked my car on the side street. Days Inn was our meeting place. The high I had experienced with him was something I needed to do one more time before I made my next move.

I fixed myself up in the car mirror before stepping out and strutting all the way to the room number he had texted to me. I knocked on the door about three to four times. Just when I turned to leave, he opened it.

"Hey, you gon' take that off?" I asked as soon as I walked into the room.

DeJuan handed me the blunt, which I knew was laced with that good stuff, and I took a pull. Instantly, I got that high that felt too good to be true.

"No, I wanted you to do it for me," he challenged as I took another pull.

I let the door close behind me as I slowly walked over to him while chewing on my bottom lip. Yeah, the shit was kicking in because DeJuan was no longer a sight to see.

I placed my hands under his shirt and pulled it over his

head. Then I let my hand trace across his stomach and travel across his dick. Grabbing the smoke from him, I took another pull. I needed to be higher than a giraffe's ass to do this. Once my body started to feel extremely loose, I knew I was high.

Going back to my mission, I unzipped his pants and pushed them down with his boxers. I turned around and pulled off my leather coat, letting it fall to the floor. I had no clothes on under it. DeJuan grabbed me and kissed my neck, sending a wave of electricity through my body just like he had done before. I grabbed the belt from my coat and wrapped it loosely around his neck. He eased himself inside me and began to pump fast.

"You make my dick feel so good," He murmured.

I had to admit his dick was nice, and it felt even better.

"You want another hit?" he questioned.

Instead of answering him, I wrapped my legs around his waist and started to match his strokes. Grabbing the smoke, I lit it and took another pull before placing it to his lips, and he did the same. I let it fall, but I wasn't sure where it went.

I raised my hips, grinding back into him as I held onto the rope and yanked it a few times. DeJuan started humping me too good for my liking.

"It fell," I tried to tell him, but DeJuan pulled out of me and then pushed back inside me, erasing the words that were about to leave my mouth.

"What was you saying?" he questioned and kissed me.

"Nothing. God, I wasn't saying nothing," I managed to get out between moans.

Hell, I didn't really remember what I was about to say.

DeJuan lifted my legs and held onto them as he pushed into me. I placed my hand on the wall and met him in the middle, stroke after stroke. This was the best dick I ever had in my life, and if it was the drugs, I wouldn't mind taking them before sex every time.

"Harder! Harder!" I urged him.

DeJuan wrapped my legs around his neck, giving himself more access to my insides. My nails were digging into the sheets as he dug into my insides.

"Oouuu. Oouu, slow down," I cried.

DeJuan was fucking the shit out of me, something I wasn't used to. When he pushed my legs further back, I placed my hands on his waist to hold him back some.

"Move your hands." He swatted my hands away and continued pounding.

"DeJuan, something is burning!" I screamed and held onto him as I came hard.

I could smell the smoke and was starting to see it. I was high but not that damn high. DeJuan was in a world of his own because he kept laying the pipe. He did a dip that had me clutching the sheets and closing my eyes. Then he slid out of me and flipped me over. My ass was in the air, and he licked back and forth between my ass and coochie, making me cum all over the place.

Finally, he picked me up, wrapping my legs around his waist as he moved us toward the bathroom. He held my hands straight against the door until I let go of his hands and wrapped my arms around his neck. I used my leg strength to help me ride him while we stood. This shit felt so good.

I grabbed the belt around his neck and pulled on it some while I moved my hips in a slow, rocking motion. He began to bounce me on him, causing my head to fall onto his shoulder. I licked and sucked on his neck as his grip on my ass cheeks tightened. He placed us on the bed, keeping one arm under me to hold me up. The burning smell was growing, and I only smelled it when we were near the bed. Assuming it as the smell from the drugs we were doing, I focused back on the sex I needed.

"Wrap your legs back," he told me, and I followed his directions.

His thrusts were now long and deep. He bit his bottom lip as he took his free hand and began to rub pearl.

"I'm about to fucking cum," I notified him, and he only humped me faster.

Grabbing the belt, I held it as tight as I could while he fucked me hard. He had his hand on my hand, and it felt like he was trying to get me off him. Just like the last time, my body locked up, and I started to cum. DeJuan stopped moving completely, which threw me off. I was exhausted, so I didn't complain about not finishing my nut.

I looked over at the window and saw a cloud of smoke along with what looked like fire. Leaning over the side of the bed, I realized the sheet was on fire. As I looked around the room, I noticed the smoke detector was unplugged.

"Get up. It's a fire." I tapped DeJuan, but he didn't move.

Panic set in my body when I called his name a few times, and he didn't say anything. I placed my finger under his nose, but I didn't feel any air coming from him. Pushing his body off mine, I quickly gathered my things and ran out of the hotel room and to my car.

Once inside the car, I sat there and watched the door. A couple of minutes went by before someone walked by and stopped at the door. At that point, smoke had started to come from under the door, and I knew if everything didn't burn up, I would be fucked.

Moments later, a fire truck pulled up. While some firefighters got out and ran to the door, the others hooked up the fire hose. I watched as they broke the window, and flames burst out. Another kicked the door down. They ran in and pulled out DeJuan's naked body. I watched them perform CPR until the paramedics pulled up. I knew once they all stood up and one came over with a white sheet that I would need to figure things out.

My phone rang, and I picked it up. Amarie was FaceTiming me. Instead of answering, I sent her to voicemail. I knew that if my cousin ever found out the truth, she would be so hurt, which was why I drove myself to the hospital, slid into the clothes I had in my car, and checked in.

"Hey, I believe someone slipped me something. I was at a bar, and I was smoking with some guy. Out of nowhere, I started feeling like I was in another world."

My plan was to meet DeJuan and have him confess to drugging me after getting him high out of his mind. It was never meant to end up like this.

"That's the girl right there from the motel, Officer," I heard a lady say as she pointed to me.

It was the same man I saw at the motel.

CHAPTER TWENTY-FOUR

AMARIE

I did my best not to show how upset I was about Nakari ignoring me. However, it had been about three days since I talked to her, and that was far too long. I was giving her space, but she wanted to disappear on everyone like she was invisible. I tried to ask Natalia about her, but every time I did, she would just steer the conversation in another direction since she felt that Nakari was doing too much. Natalia had always gotten like that when Nakari and I would get in our feelings and wanted to shut out the world. Her favorite line was, we would eventually get over it.

Climbing out of my car, I used my key to let myself into Nakari's house. It was empty, and everything was turned off. She had decorated her home with her new furniture like she said, but she wasn't home, so I left back out and locked the door. I sat in my car and dialed her number, only to get the voicemail once again. Feeling like something wasn't right, I called my auntie.

"Yeah, baby." She answered the phone, sounding like she was out of breath.

"Have you talked to Nakari?" I asked.

"Yesterday. She said she was going somewhere. I'm gon' call you back," she said and hung up. Knowing my auntie, she was somewhere getting her back blown out with her old nasty ass.

Frustrated, I drove back home. Nakari would reach out to me when she was ready, and I wasn't going to force it anymore. I hadn't done anything for her to feel like she needed to duck me.

Pulling up to the entrance of my gated community, I entered the code and drove down the path to my house. I loved the new place and could live there forever. I couldn't wait to raise my kids there and make sure they never wanted for anything. I thought about how I would have to get all the work done that I possibly could before I pushed my baby out because I refused to miss a step in my baby's life. I would be there for him or her through thick and thin. That was the promise I already made to my child, and I was going to keep it.

Pulling up into my driveway, I shut my car off before using my key to enter the house. I had taken chicken out for dinner and decided to put it in the oven before I did anything else. Going into the kitchen, I cleaned my chicken and seasoned it before placing it in a pan and covering it with chicken broth. After I was done, I placed a lid on it and slid it into the oven. I would make some white rice and string beans to go with it.

While my chicken cooked, I started my bath. After filling the tub with hot water and a few drops of bubble bath, I got in. I wanted to soak my body and relax. While in the tub, I heard my phone ring but I decided to check it later. Everyone knew if it was an emergency to call twice. When the phone didn't ring again, I knew that nothing was wrong.

Once I finished my bath, I turned the shower on and washed my body along with my hair, which hadn't been washed in weeks. The shower didn't last long since my phone rang again. As I dried myself off, I figured Nakari had come to her senses and wanted to talk. Picking up my phone, I saw an unknown number and tossed it back down. Whoever that was couldn't have wanted me because I didn't talk to people who didn't have my number.

As I lay on my bed, I turned the TV on and watched a few minutes of the news. My city was crazy. Someone was always being killed, and lately it had been more kids than adults. Once I had enough, I changed the channel just as they started talking about a fire in a rundown motel. That shit was nothing new to anyone around here. All that ever happened was these bad ass kids setting shit off.

If I had a son, I was going to make sure that he wouldn't be in the streets, and I would do my best to make him feel loved. I would let him know every day that no matter what he did in life, I would support him. I felt that most people showered their daughters with love when the sons needed it more. Men, especially black men, had it harder than anyone on the streets. That's why if I had a young black king, he would have the street smarts as well as the knowledge that he didn't have to be out there. He would only have to fight if he needed to, not because he wanted to prove himself to people. He would know that home was his place as well as mine, a place he could come to and feel safe, wanted, and loved.

I was going to make sure I talked to my kids and never missed anything, even if it was a basketball game or something simple as cheerleading practice. I would talk to my child and not at him or her. Just thinking of all the things I wanted to do with my child made me emotional.

"What's wrong, babe?" Kash asked as he walked into the room pulling his shirt off. He had a fresh cut and looked good as hell.

"Nothing. I was just watching the news, and seeing all them kids killing each other made think about all the things I would do as a parent to ensure my child took the right path in life. I hope we don't fail our child," I admitted.

"Baby, we won't. As long as we keep our family first and make sure things that are meant to be handled at home are handled at home, we'll be good. We will have to keep family out of certain business yet be open to our son or daughter reaching out to our family for things he or she don't want to come to us about, because it will happen. We can't be mad or upset about it because as we can clearly see, it takes a village." He wiped my tears away.

"What did you do today?" I asked, changing the subject.

"Man, shit, I did some light shopping for you. I took the list off the fridge and picked all that stuff up, so you don't have to. How did things go with Nakari? Did y'all talk? What's up with her?"

"No. She wasn't home, and she isn't answering my calls. I called my auntie, and she told me she had talked to her yesterday. I'm going to let her be and allow her to reach out when she's ready. I just don't want her to feel like she's alone because she's not. I feel like when I needed everybody, they were always there for me. I'm trying to be there for her as well, but she won't let me," I explained as he stripped off his outside clothes.

"Sometimes you can't force people. When she's ready to talk to you, she will. If it makes you feel better, send her a motivational message every day or simply one just letting her know you're there for her. That way, she knows you're still there, even when she's pushing everyone away. She's grieving in her own way, and maybe she's dealing with some things she hasn't told you about. Y'all are best friends. Nakari ain't gon' be on this for too long," he said and kissed me on the lips.

"Okay," I said before going back downstairs and draining my chicken to put the barbecue sauce on it.

Once that was done, I started my herb and butter rice and string beans. My phone rang, and I picked it up.

"Hello?" I placed the phone on speaker and set it on the counter.

"I'm looking for an Amarie. I believe it is," a guy's voice came through the speaker.

Kash came into the room and gave me a concerned look but didn't say anything. I shrugged to indicate that I didn't know what was going on.

"This is she," I said.

"I'm Detective Marshall, and I was calling to inform you of the passing of your husband, DeJuan Gibbs." There was a pause, and I tried to gather up words but couldn't find any.

"When did this happen?" I asked. I mean, I couldn't stand the man, but I didn't want to see him dead.

"Late last night. I tried to stop past your house, but it looked abandoned. DeJuan was in a hotel room that caught fire. I do have someone I am questioning about this incident, as he wasn't alone in the room. However, the other person made it out alive. Our fire department is investigating, and we will have more information for you soon. I'm sorry for your loss." He ended the call.

My phone beeped, and I clicked over to answer for Natalie.

"Girl, did you hear?" she yelled.

"Yeah, they just called and let me know DeJuan died in a hotel fire," I said.

"Bitch, no fucking way. Nakari is down at the police station being questioned about a fire where a guy died. She just called my mom."

My head started spinning, and my mouth went dry. There

was no way this was a coincidence. Getting up, I put my shoes on and rushed outside.

"Babe, we have to go see what's going on," I said just as my phone rang again.

I decided not to answer, but Kash did. He placed it on speaker, and the world seemed to stop as I listened to the call.

"Natalia, I swear I don't have no reason to lie. Ask Amarie. She wanted me to kill him," Nakari lied.

To be continued...

ALSO BY YONA